RHYMES *of* WHIMSY

RHYMES *of* WHIMSY

The Complete Abol Tabol

By Sukumar Ray

Translation, Analysis and Commentary by

Niladri Roy

REVISED AND ENLARGED SECOND EDITION
With original illustrations by Sukumar Ray

HATON CROSS PRESS

HATON CROSS PRESS.

Published by Haton Cross Press
Campbell, California, USA.

First published by Haton Cross Press, 2017.
Second Edition 2020.

ISBN-13: 978-0-9986557-3-4
ISBN-10: 0-9986557-3-2

To the memory of my late parents

Acknowledgements

The translator is indebted to the following individuals:

Monojit Chaudhuri for, unbeknownst to himself, having inspired this project. Goutam Biswas for encouragement to follow through with the idea and for review of the first drafts of the translations and cover text. Uday Shankar Hajra for suggestions on cover text and fonts. Susmita Sengupta for critiquing a substantial portion of the analyses. Amlan Ghosh for proof-reading the entire manuscript of the first edition. Maneish Mehrotra for editorial review of the first edition and being a general sounding-board. Angsujit Bhattacharya for scanning the public-domain images from the original illustrations for Abol Tabol.

Sushma Bana for believing in the project, unwavering support and patient hearings of multiple readings of the translated poems.

BOOK ONE
The Poems

Contents – Book One

PREFACE

Growing up, I read Sukumar Ray's Abol Tabol in the original vernacular. Translating that timeless work into English has been a privilege.

Throughout the translations, I have tried to adhere to certain self-imposed constraints that have aided in maintaining a consistent standard with regard to capturing the essence of Ray's original work. Nevertheless, a translation is but a poor shadow of the original, and I regret that I shall only be able to aspire to, but never quite succeed in completely capturing the greatness and magic of Ray's nonsense verse. Sukumar Ray's Abol Tabol is a work of genius; this translation, the product of mere competence.

It has been my humble endeavor to capture as much of the original mood, narrative, humor, rhyme and cadence as I could. It is my fervent hope that this translation will enable children, as well as adults, who do not read Bengali, to sample an imitation of some of Ray's original magic.

That, without doubt, would be the greatest reward for my labors.

This second edition includes minor revisions in translations, both for improved correspondence to their originals and enhanced reader-experience in English. It also introduces substantially revised and entirely newly discovered information in the analyses. Original illustrations by Sukumar Ray have been incorporated by popular demand, replacing those in the first edition.

Niladri Roy

San Francisco, California. February 2, 2020.

7

"Despite might nothing mean –"

Introduction to the Translated Poems

Translating Sukumar Ray's Abol Tabol presents a unique, two-fold challenge.

The simpler portion of that challenge stems from the fact that Abol Tabol relies on rhyme for much of its appeal. The more complex challenge, however, originates from the fact that Abol Tabol was not meant to be purely random verse. There is a body of evidence that suggests that most, if not all, poems in Abol Tabol carry dual meanings.

Ray so much as hints at the presence of these double meanings, via his 'bookend' poems. These are the beginning and ending poems, both titled *Abol Tabol*,* that the rest of the collection is nestled between. With the first poem, the clues that Ray embeds are very subtle; with the other one, they are easier to discern.

The term *nonsense verse* is rather broad in definition. Verse need not necessarily be 'nonsensical' or devoid of meaning in order to be classified as nonsense verse. Ray's verse does conform to the accepted definition of the category. However, inasmuch that the author intended to convey – sometimes very specific – meaning, translations need to be approached with respect for that intent.

---

*The beginning and the ending poems have been distinguished in this translation as *Rhyme of Whimsy* and *Muse of Whimsy*, respectively.

The Importance of Word-Intent

Poetry translations often focus on translating the *idea* articulated by the poet in the source language. This has the obvious benefit of communicating the essence, while simultaneously affording the translator freedom of choice in words, expressions and phrasing, to create an enjoyable reader-experience in the target language.

Translating only the obvious ideas evident in Ray's verse and relegating the original words to a position of secondary importance, however, can often lead to unintended consequences.

It may not be immediately apparent unless pointed out that *accuracy of word-intent is supremely important to the proper analysis of Ray's double-entendres* in translation. Oftentimes, previous translations have ignored this aspect and concentrated instead on translating what may have appeared to be the general intent of a line, without regard to the actual words used in the original. This has frequently resulted in the inadvertent loss of double-entendres intended by Ray.

For example, one well-known partial translation of Abol Tabol translates the Bengali

> *"Aaloy dhaka ondhokaar*
> *Ghonta baaje gondhe taar"*

in the last poem of Abol Tabol as:

> "The darkness lifts as moonshine wells
> Its sense adream with tinkling bells." [1]

This completely ignores the double meaning in these two lines. Here, Ray was also referring to the hidden satire in his poetry

– signified by 'darkness'– that is 'covered' or hidden, by 'light'. Light signifies the overt, often bright and cheerful, literal meanings of his words. Ray had never intended to say that the darkness is lifted or dispelled by light. He meant that the darkness that he has hidden in his poems is concealed by light, and he wrote, literally, exactly that.

Rhyme and Responsibility

With great rhyme comes great responsibility. Ray's poems superbly utilize rhyme to create a significant portion of their charm. His rhyming schemes, quite expectedly, vary. For example, in *Hookah-Face Hyangla* Ray uses the Spanish Sestet or Sextilla *a.a.b.c.c.b.* in each stanza. In other poems, he has used more complex schemes like the Violette: *a.a.a.b.c.c.c.b.* where *b* is the linking rhyme from stanza to stanza.

It is the responsibility of the translator to ensure that the rhyme is preserved in translation.

The translator also bears the responsibility of ensuring that reader-experience in the target language not be adversely affected in the process of preserving rhyme. The use of unusual grammatical constructs and obscure or even 'invented' words (as observed in some translations of Abol Tabol), simply for the sake of rhyme, is best avoided. So should be the practice of changing the rhyming scheme altogether. Clearly, these constraints too contribute to the challenge of translation.

Cadence, Tempo and Meter

Ray's use of cadence and tempo is usually consistent with his narrative. In the first poem of Abol Tabol he uses a lilting, rhythmic cadence and a reasonably fast-paced tempo to conjure up a vision of the feast of rhymes as well as of whimsy to come. In other poems his cadence is more balladic, such as when telling a long story at a lively pace, as in *Once Bitten Twice Shy*.

In the last poem of Abol Tabol he abruptly switches tempo halfway through the poem, from the slow and melodic to the quick and bright, before slowing down again for the last couple of lines, with devastating effect.

Ray's meter is primarily iambic but the dactyl, too, is evident in poems like *(M)address* and *Learning Science*. Preservation of original meter is next to impossible in poetry translations. Cadence however, if managed well, can result in the meter of the translated work being close enough to the original to be almost indistinguishable from it.

The poems that follow were translated with the above constraints of word-intent, rhyme, cadence and meter in mind. Sometimes, though, it has not been possible to adhere to all of them simultaneously in every poem. The effort, nevertheless, has been to be as 'responsible' as possible while creating a pleasurable reader-experience in the English language.

THE POEMS

Pippin boater
Pumpkin floater
Marlins in scabbard.
Built a wigwam
Father William
For Mother Hubbard.

- N.R.

Rhyme of Whimsy

Come all ye, here carefree,
Sail your little dreamboat
O'er crazy rhymes and fun times
And drumbeats of wild note.

Where merry mad song trills all day long,
Sans sense and sans tune;
Where wild winds sing; the mind takes wing,
O'er some distant sand dune.

Come mindless, be boundless,
Dance a jolly jig and trot.
Come unruly, cajole and bully
The rule books this world's got.

Be Bohemian. And Contrarian,
Your wild side, come, here nurse;
Come ye muddled, to a world befuddled
In impossible whimsy verse.

Mutant Medley

Was a duck; porcupine* (grammar I defy),
Turned to Duckpine; know not how or why.

Stork said to turtle, "Behold! Though bizarre,
Looks quite fabulous our Storktle avatar!"

The parrot-face lizard is worried just silly,
Must it quit bugs now and eat green chili?

The goat, in a stealthy plot that he hatched,
Jumped the scorpion; head 'n torso matched!

To roaming the wilds, giraffe said goodbye;
Will take flight now on wings of dragonfly.

The cow wailed, "Am I losing my mind?
There's a raging rooster on my behind!"

Whale of Whalephant would take to water;
Elephant opined: "The jungle is better!"

The Leghorn[†], for horns did mope and pine;
With a pair from the deer he's now just fine!

---

* This unusual construct was chosen by Sukumar Ray himself. For a brief discussion, see analysis in Book Two of this volume.

† The Leghorn hen, with horns borrowed from the deer, was actually a lion with deer-horns, rather than a hen, in the Bengali original. The species was changed in the translation in order to derive an acceptable name of a creature, that conveys the concatenation of the body and horns of two different species. Ray's original choice of name is, unfortunately, not translatable into intelligible English. Ray's original illustration, reproduced above, depicts a lion with head and horns of a deer, and, sadly, will not agree with the translated verse.

Knotty Woodoo

Bearded old man hunched over crockpot,
Sun-basks, licking up wet wood stew hot.
Humming a merry song, bald pate sunlit;
One would think he must be a pundit!

Mutters to himself – makes sense not so good:
"Sky-hung cobwebs cause knots in wood."
Bald pate hot gets; breaks in deep sweat;
"They just don't get it!" he gripes, in sad fret:

"Asses! A prize herd! Clueless rabble!
Good for nothing but endless squabble.
Know not which sap what type wood takes;
Why soon new moon knots in wood makes?"

Charts and figures and drawn up long lists;
Cracked wood, driftwood, countless, he insists.
Which crack tastes good, which just so-so,
Which scents, for sure, with which clefts go.
Wood on wood clacks cacophony rap-mix;
"I know which knocks what sort woods fix!

Messed with rough woods; this I know sure:
Which tough treatments rogue woods do cure.
Which wood gets tamed, which is peaceful;
Which wood anemic and which is a pit-bull.
Which wood, naïve fool, can't true from false tell
Which woods have knots, know why full well."

Mouche Filch

Head Clerk at head office, a man quiet and peaceful
Who knew that his head harbored an ailment so awful?
One moment happy, content and tranquil at desk sit,
Dozed in peace; without notice, suddenly just lost it!

Popped eyeballs, gave a start, let fly a high kick,
Shrieked he, "Woe! I'm a goner! Help me up real-quick!"
Some called the medicine-man, some yelled for cops
Some warned still, "He might bite! Do mind your chops!"

Ran 'round busy, in a fair tizzy, all clueless as to role
Head Clerk barked, "Listen up now – my moustache is stole!"
A stolen mouche? What notion strange! Could that be right?
The luxuriant pair seems all there – harmed not the slight.

"You're Ok!" they assured him – even held up a mirror,
"Mouche never gets filched, you know, you're surely in error."
Head Clerk – face beetroot red – fuming and furious
Raged, "I don't trust you lot – not a bounder's serious!"

"Uneven cut; a broomstick but! So soiled and so grimy,
Shyam Babu's milkman had a moustache this slimy.
Call this mine? How dare you! You deserve to be shot!"
So said he – and in vengeful spree – fined all on the spot.

In sputtering rage, vexed visage, he wrote in the big book:
"Give 'em an inch – they take a mile; fact not to overlook.
Bunch of loons – stupid baboons – craniums threadbare,
Where – alas – my moustache went, nobody gives a care!
How I wish from these rascals' own moustaches to swing!
Take a big spade, scrape their pates till all hair takes wing.
Mouche they call 'mine/yours' – like mouche you just buy?
Mouche owns you, mouche owns me: It defines the guy!"

Prize Groom

Heard this, when to *Posta* I got –
Your daughter is tying the knot?
Ganga Ram the auspicious match?
Care to learn what sort of catch?

Not bad at all – he's really bright –
Complexion, like the moonless night;
Handsome he, of face and jowl
Would put to shame a scowling owl.

Brains, you ask? Let me tell you –
For dogged grit, set records anew!
After nineteen tries of matching his wits
At passing school, he called it quits.

What of his means? Poor deadbeat –
Struggles just to make ends meet.
A pair of brothers not worth scrap –
One village idiot, the other madcap.

A third is clever, sharp as a nail;
Forged banknotes and went to jail.
The youngest plays gigs onstage;
As often as not, doesn't get paid.

Ganga Ram is often sick with fever;
Pale and jaundiced, distended liver.

But their family is of a lofty line:
Of *Kangsha*, the tyrant king divine!
Infamous* *Shyam* of *Bonogram*
Is related somehow to *Ganga Ram*.

Key thing is, you've snagged a groom;
A prize catch; for doubt, little room!

---

* "Infamous *Shyam*" is '*Shyam Lahiri*' in the original. This translator has been unable to unearth contemporaneous references to this particular gentleman. It is an educated guess that he may have been infamous.

Butting Muse

Belting along a summer song, *Vishmalochan Sharma*
In fulsome noise assaults the sense, Delhi to Burma.
Croons like there's no tomorrow, yodels up a grand din;
People run hither-tither, their heads all in a tailspin.

A multitude comes unglued, all injured and crying:
"Stop that noise! Be quick now! Surely, I'm dying!"
Unbridled cattle and horse tumble by wayside;
Vish drones on, in oblivion, un-stemmed his song-tide.

Heavenward four hooves pointed, poor beasts fall senseless,
Tail stuck high, mutter half-crazed, "Darn it – it's endless!"
The sea-dwelling – surprising – are quiet in deep redoubt;
Strong trees just snap like twigs; a generation wiped out.

Birds in flight, twisters fight, turn cartwheels in the air;
All implore, ad nauseam, encore, "Stop! Stop!" in despair.
Rising clamor the heavens shakes, cracks concrete edifice,
Vish still coos, in blissful muse, nary a thought of dismiss.

A mad billy-goat, of song took note; felt offended, unkind,
Gathered horn in withering scorn; head-butted *Vish* behind.
And that was that! That's all it took – the awful din to kill;
"Ow! I'm gone!" yelled *Vishmalochan* – and all was still.

The illustration, which appears here in greyscale, was a full-page color plate – the only illustration in color – in the original Bengali first edition of Abol Tabol.

The Contraption

A contraption very curious built *Chandidas'* uncle;

Bravo! said the young, and the old of sage wrinkle.

When Uncle had been but a babe, hardly a year-old,

His sudden cry of "Goonga", stopped everyone cold.

Others gurgle, 'Mama', 'Gaga', nonsense and rot;

This child coos, 'Goonga!' What a marvelous tot!

All agreed: "Should this kid live to be a man,

Make a name for himself in the world he sure can."

Uncle, of infant-fame, has made a device so clever,
Five-hour trips in ninety minutes it'll readily deliver.
I took a look, the apparatus is straightforward and simple;
You'd grasp it in five hours without raising a pimple.

Inner workings – what can I say! For words, I'm at a loss;
It straps around one's neck like the Mariner's Albatross.*
From a beam up front swings fragrant food of your fancy,
Chops, cutlets or spiced samosas of delicious pungency.

To take a bite of such invite, as you would neck stretch,
In miming move, dangling food would move ahead a step.
And thus lured to chase fabulous feasts of your taste,
The gadget ensures that, motivated, you pursue posthaste.

Leagues you'd cover by the dozen, and notice not at all;
Whiffs enticing, trail unwavering, in ardent footfall.

Said all in one voice: young, and the old of sage wrinkle,
"An achievement unparalleled leaves *Chandidas'* uncle!"

---

* Admittedly, the reference to "Mariner's Albatross" (from *The Rime of the Ancient Mariner* by Samuel Coleridge) could have been avoided, and a simpler analogy used. However, the opportunity for dark humor that it provided was too tempting to pass up.

Battle Crazed

Ah! There goes our crazy *Jagai* – comes here every day,
Hums himself his private tune; to himself smiles away.
Makes like he's about to walk, then suddenly stops short;
Hops right to left in swift sidestep, quick bound and trot.

In great vehemence rolls up sleeves 'n gathers up attire,
Yells, 'Yahoo!', then bunches fist and pokes it in the air.
Hollers, "Set a trap, have you? Think *Jagai* would fall?
Seven Huns* 'gainst one *Jagai*; yet *Jagai* takes on all."

Dances, hot in keen excitement; a veritable jumping jack;
Charges ahead at certain times, at other times pulls back.
Rolled umbrella he whacks about in haphazard strokes;
Twirls around in effortless style, like spinning fireworks.

Breathless and dripping sweat from many a leap and bound,
With almighty thud drops prostrate, down onto the ground.
Flings arms and legs about; with glazed eyes cries, anon –
"Poor *Jagai* is dreadful-dead, from sudden shot of cannon!"

Having cried thus, and for a minute having fidgeted violent,
Makes like the dead, stiff as a board; goes absolutely silent.
Then sits up ramrod straight, and scratches his head some,
Fishing from his pocket out an accountants' ledger tome.

In that he wrote, "Listen, *Jagai*, a great battle transpired;
Finishing off five rogues first, *Jagai* The Great expired."

Caution

Stop! Stop! Desist, now, Victor Delgado,[*]
Pant not so hard you whip up a tornado!
Know not, last year, Pablo next floor,
Breathed hard, almost was at death's door?

Gasp not so loud through your big mouth;
What if bugs fly straight down it south?
Ricardo's uncle – the one from Madeira,
Ate a fly, months five, suffered from cholera.

Careful, therefore, make but no sound;
Pass through silent, tippy-toe, homebound.
Look not left-right, wander or yaw;
Caution saves lives – such writes in law.

Recall the poor chap from the fables of yore?
Going his merry way, down a well fell, sore?

Ah! One more thing: mornings 'n noonday,
Bathe not - not ever - in pond or pool may;
A figure this plump – you never know when...
It's all rather precarious – I'm sure you ken.

Why get annoyed? Who knows for sure,
If bad stuff befalls, what you might endure?

Don't just argue some silly nonsense junk;
Have some respect, you, smarty-pants punk!

You heed not advice on movement or meal;
With a rude awakening, might one day deal.
Miguel's uncle – he a man ever so guileful,
Of all my sage advice, never was mindful.
One day at market, having gone to buy roast,
Got run-over mid-street and gave up the ghost!

---

* Bengali names of people and of a place have been replaced with Latin American or Spanish names. In the original Bengali poem, Ray had relied, several times, on the use of actual names of people, for the sake of rhyme. In other words, he exercised certain liberties by inserting people-names that would rhyme with the rest of his verse. This translator found it expedient to assume the same liberty and used Latin American names to resolve the same issues in the translation.

Shadow Play

Not fantasy nor fairy tale, 'tis the truth, to be sure,
From wrestling a shadow, my poor frame is sore.

Ply a trade in shadows I; don't you know that story?
Sun-shadows and moon shadows; varied inventory!
Dawn shadows, sleek and fresh, new in dew wetted;
Summer-shadows, crispy-fried, sunburnt, desiccated.
Hawks that at hot high noon fly circles in the sky,
Set traps on their soaring shadows; snare in cages I.
Crow-shadows and stork – a myriad have I picked;
Bland ones of cloud-wisps too, I've got them licked.
None realize, nor can fathom – not by a long chalk;
None can stalk shadows as I, pursue round the clock.

Think you would, tree-shadows just lie down aground,
Looking like they're fast asleep, peaceful and sound?

The real story, if you wish to know, just you ask me;
The absolute truth, without doubt, I tell you, verily:
When they perceive no one's about; not a soul in glance,
Cautiously peer here and there – look about askance.
That's when you creep up behind, that's when to risk it:
Jump up sudden, spring your trap, stuff 'em in a basket.

Dark shadows 'n light shadows, shadows without fetter;
In comparison with actual trees, tree-shadows are better.
Herbs, barks, shoots, roots, saplings: remedies futile;
Shadow-meds make ailments cry "Uncle"; run a mile.
He who imbibes bitter shadows of *Neem* bark and more,
Good night's sleep begets he in deep sonorous snore.
Papaya-shadow, by moonlight, if you snag off the tree,
One sniff, and of cold and cough, forever would be free.
Dirty shades of hog-plum tree, if they bite and chew out,
The disabled sprout a pair of legs, that's beyond a doubt.
Desirous from damp sickness of monsoon rains escape?
Doses of hot tamarind shadow, for a week or three take.

Sweet shades o' *Mahua* tree, with a blotter I soak up;
Squeeze 'em out, real careful, in ampoules lock up.
Downright new, fresh treatment – purely indigenous;
Priced them real cheap a vial: just fourteen *annas.**

---

* The *anna* was a denomination of coin. Its value was one-sixteenth
   of the Indian Rupee, the monetary unit in British India.

Pumpkin-Pudge

(Should) Pumpkin-Pudge dance –
Beware! On no account, must stable-wards advance;
Look not right, nor to the left; don't backwards glance;
Dangle from a loft-radish bough, in four-leg-upend stance.

(Should) Pumpkin-Pudge cry –
Beware! Beware! A rooftop-perch mustn't even try;
Bundle up in blankets, lie prone on a hammock high;
In melodies of *Bihag,** endless, *Radhe Krishna Radhe*[†] sigh.

(Should) Pumpkin-Pudge laugh –
By the kitchen, on one leg, stay standing like a staff;
In hushed tones speak Persian; breath bated by half;
Fast three meals – nope, no appeal – lie on grass-chaff.

(Should) Pumpkin-Pudge run –
Double-quick, up windowsill, scramble everyone;
In red-rouged *hookah*-water, douse your cheeks overdone;
Make sure again, by mistake even, skywards look none.

(Should) Pumpkin-Pudge call –
Rondelles on heads tightly fixed, ride bathtubs all;
On foreheads apply spinach-paste, like rubbing-alcohol;
With hot pumice of very hard brick, scrub noses overall.

If you think this too trivial and pay not any heed,
Once Pumpkin-Pudge finds out, it's comeuppance indeed!
You'll realize then, I promise you, as my sayings prove right,
Don't blame me then. Don't say that I gave you no foresight.

---

*Bihag is the name of a *raga* or melodic mode in Indian classical music.

†A religious chant invoking the name of the Hindu god *Krishna* and his consort *Radha*.

Owl and Owlin

Owl says Owlin –
Nice caterwaulin'.

In dulcet cadences –
My soul fair prances.

Throaty, delightful,
Your serenade soulful.

Shrill note hard rife,
Startles plant life.

Tunes twine tangled,
In melodies mangled.

All sorrow, all dread
All fearful tread,

With your tunes, yet,
I clean forget.

Comely, sweet cries,
Mist up my eyes.

Tickling Old-Timer

Wander across the seven seas, go you will wherever,
Of Tickling Old-Timer beware, avoid him forever.
Perilous old person he is – never at home visit;
His tickly tricks will surely knit your guts all in a twist.

No one's sure where he lives; the crossing of which streets,
You'll be forced to hear, caught unaware, stories that he bleats.
Very wacky his yarns are too – absurd and awry;
Instead of being amused, you'll far more likely cry.
Neither head nor tail have they, nor do they have meaning;
Pretend you must to like them still; at old man grinning.

Were it just tales he told, maybe one could weather,

But tickles you he, on top of it, using a long feather.

Says he ceaseless: "Ho! Ho! Ho! *Kestodas'* aunt,

Used to sell duck-eggs and pumpkins and plant.

The eggs were all long in shape, the pumpkins but bent;

Around the plants multi-colored patterns in paint went.

Round the clock sang this aunt like a donkey at bray,

Meow meow wackum wackum wuf wuf wuf neigh."

And, so saying, he leaps up sudden and pinches your nape;

Lunges with a skinny finger, your ribs to poke and scrape.

Tickles you thus, but himself laughs, rolling on the floor;

Until you laugh with him, there's no getting out the door.

Derelict Shack

Smiling broadly, wolfing a rice snack,
Grizzled old woman in her derelict shack.

Cobwebby blanket, hair covered in dust,
Back-bent, eyes rheumy in the color of rust.
The nailed-up, glue-taped old hut, decrepit,
Holds up makeshift string-ties spit-licked.

A lean-to(o)* precarious: lean, and it might fall,
Cough too loud and it shakes in close call.

Honks if carriage or hawks street-vendor,
Tumble rafters – shack crashes asunder.

Askew chambers, all hollow amidships,
Sweep, and it rains down a hail of wood chips,
Wet with rain, the roof gets sag-prone,
Props up with sticks, herself, the old crone

Repairs copious must day and night track,
Grizzled old woman in her derelict shack.

---

*This translator initially meant to simply use 'lean-to', in the normal dictionary definition of such a structure, but found the opportunity of a simultaneous allusion to 'too precarious' too tempting to pass up; hence lean-to(o).

The Quack

Come over, check out doctor brilliant –
Cut, scrape, break, sprain repaired instant.
Advised mentor: "Listen, Apprentice,
Cut up paper dolls first, for practice."
Zest and effort when keen zeal infects,
One knows, of course, practice perfects.

In medical-learning I am battle-scarred,
Over time figured, the art's not too hard.
Scissors, scalpel, tools and know-how,
Broke-bone make-whole, all I've learnt now.
Cut up, effortless, big effigies, gleeful,
The more I slice; the more am cheerful.

Cut throats and legs; hands and chest,
Quick-set wood-glue puts back best.
Time to treat now real patients live –
You, *Bhola*, go out and fetch me five!

Suffers from arthritis our Mr. *Nandy,*
Avoids treatment; offer threat or candy.
One day soon, I plan to him here lure,
Artfully operate, and his arthritis cure.

Cold, cough, earache – pain no factor,
Come here, fear not, I'm the doctor.
Who's that lying down? Busted leg?
Bring here; fixed with screw and peg!

What ails you now? Have a toothache?
Tap of a hammer 'n I prompt well make.
Couple teeth this side, three on the other –
Pluck with pliers, I – teeth no bother.

Old patient or young; blind or lame,
Cholera or dengue – the cure is the same.
Fresh or chronic; black-fever or yellow,
Arrests instant, an astute hammer-blow!

Wacky No-One

Wacky that animal: very weird jumble,
All day long, does ceaseless grumble.
Field and stream he roams in complain,
Whines fair frightful in constant refrain:
"Need this, want that –", always pining,
What really he wants, defeats divining.

Wants, like a bird, to croon in sweet tweet,
Of his voice own, claims, "It's downbeat!"
Birds fly unfettered up blue sky high,
Sad that he lacks wings, settles down to cry.

Grand looks elephant in tusk and trunk sage,
Demands the same be bolt on his visage.
Kangaroo's leaps turn him envious green,
Such legs must have, all lanky and lean.

Lion's mane, why, he lacks, so ferocious?
Why not serrated lizard-tail, curvaceous?
Only all of that would sate his yearning
Laments to all: "Look! I'm in mourning!"

Finally, for long having cried and ranted,
Magically happened, the thing he wanted.
Mourning forgot; in delight intoxicated,
Sat quietly alone and long ruminated:

Does an elephant jump *whoosh* up high?
On a diet of plantains, do kangaroos die?
Can tweeting birdcalls, a face like this grace?
Does trunk on body such, look out of place?
Airborne old elephant, if accepts no one?
If they box his ears, twist tail, make fun?
Charges someone straight to his face:
"Who're you, bud? What name, what race?"
How to respond? How such doubts foil?
Sits sheepishly troubled, his mind in turmoil –

"Am not horse, scorpion, reptile or elephant,
Bee nor butterfly – or winged coelacanth!
Fish, frog, shrubbery, earth, sea, wave, none;
Not shoes or umbrella, I must be No-One!"

To Catch a Thief

Disgraceful, I tell you! Do be aware,
Con-games, rampant, beyond compare!

Soon as I take my nap, pre-lunch,
Wake up to portions reduced a bunch.
Food purloined – my daily misery,
Yesterday surpassed highway robbery.
Burgers, five, I had on a plate,
Breadsticks 'n pizza, topped cheese grate.
Piled atop were fritters aplenty –
Woke up to find, my plate was empty!

Am sore, therefore; can one take more?
Borne enough yet; must now even score.
Day-long, hence, I stand guard, watchful,
Will catch, for sure, food-thieves, deceitful.

Whoever you might be, Tom, Dick or Harry[*] –

Once apprehended you're going to be sorry!

Trickery, treachery or guile yours futile,

Soon as I catch you, will punish you in style.

Here I wait hid, ready baseball-bat,[†]

Just you rear head – will bring down pat.

Warnings, daily, still falling on deaf ears?

Try once more – you'll meet your worst fears!

---

* "Tom, Dick or Harry" has been used in place of Bengali names to keep the translation idiomatically, rather than literally, accurate – which was necessary to preserve the intended meaning of the original.

† "Baseball bat" is an obvious western reference, which seemed an appropriate mechanism to avoid potential references of violence involving bloodshed. Ray's original illustration, reproduced above, shows a sword, in keeping with the original verse. Several food names, too, have been westernized, to aid in rhyming.

It's All Good

Hear ye! Methought far 'n with this I came up –

In this world, is all good.
Real is good, unreal good.

Cheap is good; and dear, good.
I am good – and you are good.

Here, sing-song cadences good.
Sweet smelling flower-scents good.

Cloud-decked, the welkin good.
The wind is surf-raisin' good.

Winter's good, summer is good.
Dark is good and fair is good.

Curries are good 'n fried-rice good.
Fish 'n veggies are with spice good.

Raw is good, ripened good.
Straight is good, twisted good.

Gongs are good, drumbeats good.
Cowlicks good; bald pates good.

Pushcarts, to push are good.

Bruschetta, to brush are good.

Bold tenor is for listenin' good.

And cotton-wool, to gin is good.

Cool water is for a bath good.

But none better the world hath good,

Than pancake and maple syrup.*

---

*Readers familiar with the original Bengali work may be able to appreciate that the names of the foods '*pauruti* and *jholagur*' in the original can present a translation challenge. Translating literally to 'bread and molasses' or 'bread and jaggery' did not appear to fit too well; hence, the decidedly western pancake and maple syrup. Several other food names have been westernized to aid in rhyming.

Note: It is interesting to note the original rhyming scheme (which has been preserved in translation). Apart from the first and last lines, the *penultimate* word of each line rhymes with the penultimate word of the following line. The last words of the first and last lines rhyme with each other.

What a Surprise!

Hey! Heard tell that the old druid – of yon, yonder seat,

Gathers mouthfuls with his hands as he sits down to eat?

And hungry he gets when he hasn't eaten all day?

Eyelids close on their own should sleep come his way?

His feet touch the ground whenever he walks?

Hears with his ears, all? With eyes, at all gawks?

His noggin's by his head when in slumber he sprawls?

Let's go see how it really is; is all that true or false?

Babu - The Snake-Charmer

Babu Snake-Charmer – Where do you wander?

Sit down two shakes* – Put up two snakes

Snakes with no tails – No horns, no nails

Run not, nor fight – Or anyone bite

Those that don't hiss – Nor hit or miss

Snakes that play nice – Eat milk and rice

Such snakes supple – Bring me a couple!

I'll make so bold – (As) To knock 'em out cold.[†]

---

*Two shakes: a short while. As "In two shakes of a lamb's tail."

[†]The ending has been changed in order to reduce reference to cruelty to animals. Today, the majority of readers appreciates that not all snakes are dangerous and need not be exterminated as a rule.

King of *Bombagarh*

Know you why King of realm by *Bombagarh* name,
Fried mango-wafers keeps tucked in a photo frame?
To tie a pillow to her head why does queen bother?
Nails hammer in loaves of bread, her elder brother?
Why folks there, for cold-remedy, turns-turtle ply?
On moonlit nights, red-rouged kohl to their eyes apply?
Experts, their heads and necks cover up with quilts?
Postage stamps, on their bald pates stick all pundits?

Nighttime, their pocket-watches dip people in lard?
The king makes his bed, why, on sandpaper-card?
At audience, why does the king like a jackal yap?
Prime minister drums on a pot sitting on king's lap?
Broken bottles hung on throne, why does king flaunt?
With a pumpkin play cricket, why does king's aunt?
King's uncle – wreathed in smoke-pipes, dances he?
Why is all this happening, now, can someone tell me?

Word-fancy-*boughoom!**

Bang! Bang! Boom! Blast! What was that?
Sunbursts bloom? Thought fireworks crack!
"Puff-puff! Pant-pant!" this isn't fun –
The blossom's yellow, but the colors run!

Thump! Thwack! Whup! Whack! Woe, what dread!
It's the falling dew; please mind your head.
"Glub! Glub! Gloop!" in drowning swoon,
Westward sinks dawn's pale half-moon.

With a clink of coins the night is spent
Whoosh! By rocket-ship wake up went.
Buzz! Buzz! Spins thought in my head
Thud! Thud! Soul-dance feet of lead.

"Growl! Snort! Snarl!" in roaring pain,
'Crack!' breaks my heart but in vain.
"Hoodle 'um! Hoodle 'um!" rises cry[†]
Hoodlums approach? It's time to fly!

---

*Literal meanings have been changed from the original in most cases in order to preserve the intent of the original work, which was to humorously relate words for everyday sounds (onomatopoeia) to the *literal* meanings of (often unrelated) idiomatic expressions. See detailed commentary in Book Two, later in this volume.

†This translator found it satisfyingly fitting to use the word 'hoodlum' which entered the English language through a pseudo-onomatopoeic route. "Hoodle 'um!" is probably 'Huddle 'em', spoken with a thick Irish brogue. The word originated in San Francisco, probably from a particular street-gang's call to unemployed Irishmen to "huddle 'em" (to beat up Chinese migrants), after which San Francisco newspapers took to calling street gangs 'hoodlums'. This information has often been erroneously attributed to Herbert Asbury. However, while he discussed several alternative origins of the word in his book, Asbury never specifically claimed the above to be correct.[2]

Note: Some alternative dictionary definitions of hoodlum, attributing it to probably dialectal German, are almost certainly incorrect. Compare Swabian derivatives of Hudel: rag, e.g. hudelum: disorderly, hudellam: weak, slack; Hudellump: rags, slovenly, careless person, and related words in other dialects, that indicate 'untidy', rather than 'ruffian'.

Once Bitten Twice Shy*

Sunburnt bricks piled up neat
      On this King takes a seat
Bagful o' peanuts proceeds to eat
      But swallows them not.
Wearing warm wool jerkin
      Hot sun his back burnin'
Says King, "Get a downpour in,
      Else all's going to pot."

Perches there all afternoon
      Quiet in self-spun cocoon
Long-faced in silent gloom
      Clutching his little slate.

Bathed he in sweat profuse

 Befuddled in lone recluse

Writes stuff that all confuse

 Its meaning none can state.

Merciless the midday sun

 Drills open his head undone

Dance within his brain and churn

 Swirls of boiling blood.

Hot noonday air searing

 Says King, "I'm all done in!

Quick, get some ice brought in;

 I don't feel so good."

Alarmed, gather all a-scurry

 Opine: "King dies of worry!

O King, please do answer query,

 Why are you so?

Ruddy face as dry desiccated

 As old parchment resuscitated

Why King's so hot and sweated,

 We've a right to know!"

Says King "Does anyone care

 To solve a problem, I despair;

Tell you all fair and square –

 I'll let my thought out.

Listen to what I have to tell,

    Ponder even you as well;

Answer none that rings any bell.

    It's a veritable rout.

Says in books of learning high

    'Once bitten, twice is shy.'

Question that has no reply

    Is 'why twice, not more?'

From eons old to now further,

    Understood none neither;

Doesn't say in books either.

    No one knows for sure.

Be they shy times one million,

    Can threat or gold bullion

Stop any silly rapscallion

    That's really determined?"

As soon as King this had said,

    Up popped a child his head.

Said, "King, with all I've read,

    I've made up my mind.

Perusing as I have done,

    Many a weighty learned tome;

Reflecting on 'em very hard some,

    Found a way to hack

A solution elegant and clever;

Time-tested, will stand forever:

Bitten once, one shy is *never,*

If one but bites back!"

---

* This translation represents some very clear deviation from the narrative towards the end, although it does preserve the bulk of it. The deviation was imperative because most of the humor in the original poem hinges upon interpreting the Bengali saying *Nera Beltolaay, etc.* of the original title, *Nera Beltolaay Jaay Kobaar?* in the *literal* rather than the idiomatic sense.

The title translates, idiomatically, in English to "Once Bitten Twice Shy." Since, the Bengali title was interpreted literally, for the sake of humor, the same had to be done with the English equivalent (Once Bitten, etc.). The two sayings, in Bengali and English, while idiomatically of identical meaning, are obviously quite different when taken literally; hence the unavoidable deviation.

As to the nature of the deviation, this poem is obviously about British rule in India (see analysis in Book Two, later in this volume). It is this translator's belief that Ray, as a nationalist, would have loved the child's response, since, "The limits of tyrants are prescribed by the endurance of those whom they oppress." – Frederick Douglass.

Explanations

Hey, *Shyamadas,* come here, you! Sit here a moment,
I'll explain that thing vital in five minutes of comment.

You're ill you say? That's a lie! Just plain old trickery –
Heard you laugh a whole lungful a while ago in mockery.
Your uncle sick? Fetching a medic? Fetch him afternoon,
Or perhaps, *I* can suggest a way to make him well soon.
Determined today am I that you comprehend sans fail,
Even if in your noggin I must hammer it in with a nail.

What stuff, you ask? Clean forgot? Blew it out your mind?
What'd I tell you, night before last, when last we aligned?
Oh, great! So you didn't forget; harm any in repeating?
Yet it seems you run away from it; behavior self-defeating!

What's the hurry – a minute tarry – come here, sit a while –
The young these days – impatient ways – to reason with, futile.

What's that, now? Don't just sit! Bring down those books,
When you're around, lift loads I – likely that looks?
Careful now – let me help; Darn! You've got me sweating!
No, not the thesaurus, stupid! Won't need that for working.
Enough already! Desist now – sit yourself down there,
Hey, *Gopal,* go ask *Khendi* to send some snacks up here.

Let's see, as orbs of matter from fine to coarse transform,
Thrust build-up in roots of the five elements is the norm.
So, one must check, at the outset, from where and how,
Collects sap in the roots of this chimerical world-bough.
That means – just suppose now – a sunlit grass-patch,
Suppose also, a moonbeam-sliver juxtaposed to match ...

Just look at you! What do you mean by already yawning?
Wayward, keep looking skyward; is any sense dawning?
What did you say? That this is all just stuff and nonsense?
To appreciate – I reiterate – needs someone less dense.
A headful of dry cow-dung is what you have for brain,
Useful stuff to therein insert, one attempts but in vain –

Hey, *Shyamadas,* why getting up? Forever want to run!
You never listen, yet come bug me; think that this is fun?
Knowledge falls on deaf ears, yell how much one might –
Punish, I wish, could these rascals – screw their ears tight.

Hookah-Face *Hyangla*

Hookah-Face *Hyangla*   Makes home *Bangla*
   No smile on his face so grim
What does that mean?   Can anyone glean?
   Was ever one close by him?

His uncle *Shyamadas*   Drug-cop top brass
   Is all he has to hold dear
Perhaps therefore,   Face pale, sad, sore
   Alone he sits close a-tear?

Thump-thump plump feet   He used to dance beat
   Used to frolic and scamper
Day-long sang song   Do-re-mi-fa ting-tong
   Gleeful, glad happy camper.

Just this afternoon   He sat on a pontoon
   Eating mashed bananas raw
Did he sprain his ankle?   Did he lose his uncle?
   Cause other, for sudden gloom, one saw?

Hookah-Face honks out,   "Not those – not a doubt,
   See, with worry I am troubled?
This strategy to swat flies   The more my mind tries
   The more is in vexation redoubled.

If right side a fly took   It says in my book
      Should swat it I with this tail
If it should sit left   With left-hook deft
      Of this other tail, it nail.

But if it perchance   Sits middle, askance
      I can think not what to do –
I'm all a-confuse   Which tail to use
      Have no more tail but two!"

The Twenty-One Law

In God's Own Country charming,

The laws are quite alarming!

If someone should slip and fall,

The king's footmen pay a call.

Tries the offender a magistrate –

      Twenty-one bucks fine straight.

Evenings, before six, it's writ,

To sneeze, one must have a ticket.

Without ticket if you sneeze –

Must step down on your knees.[*]

Up your nose blows snuff someone –

      Makes you sneeze, times twenty-one.

---

*Some elements have been changed to avoid what might potentially have been classified as police brutality.

Suffer if you from a loose tooth,

Pay four bucks duty at the booth.

Happen you to a moustache grow,

A hundred *annas** tax you owe –

That's not all, in compliance mute,

        Must twenty-one times salute.

Walking, should someone sight,

Here and there, left and right,

Immediate, they the king inform,

Jump up his men in uniform.

Make you sweat in the noonday sun,

        Drink water, ladles twenty-one.

Those people who poetry write,

Get locked up in cages tight.

In discordant tunes varied,

Math tables in their ears they read.

In audit of grocers' accounts engages

        Make them tally twenty-one pages.

There, if sudden past midnight deep,

You happen to snore in your sleep,

They charge in and rub your head in haste,

With wood-apple and cow-dung paste.

Twenty-one times spin you around

        Hang twenty-one hours off the ground.

---

*Denomination of coin, one-sixteenth of the British-Indian *Rupee*.

Ding-a-ling and Dong

Running motors, spinning rotors, hackney carriage bustling,
Hurrying people scurrying about – each their own hustling.
Hurtling amok a multitude – tempting fate in traffic,
Tourists* stare in consternation – a scene chaotic graphic!
We however, staunch endeavor to drum a delightful song:
"Ding-a-ling and dong!"

Monsoon rains drench the city, streets covered in mud,
Of cold and flu on chilly wet nights, why take risk, bud?
No matter if it be morning, evening; no matter afternoon,
Matters not affairs of office or work piled up to the moon.
Moonlit night, come, hear us delight – serenade in song:
"Ding-a-ling and dong!"

Dimwits are they who sit all alone; heads buried in books,
Plain bewildered or wearing rather vacant, sheepish looks.
Some are lost in boundless worry; crestfallen in wake.
Sit around like a bunch of fools, their heads endless shake.
Better if you dare, to toss all care, and with us sing along:

> "Ding-a-ling and dong!"

Going about your way dispirited, your time you so fritter,
Walk many miles, work countless whiles, in silence suffer.
Crux crucial, you just don't get – not thinking on your feet,
Don't you hear, in refrain clear, thrums a beckoning beat?
In sustained rigor, with redoubled vigor, join us in song:

> "Ding-a-ling and dong!"

---

*"Tourists stare in consternation" is a deviation from the original.
The original contained a reference to British settlers – a common
sight in urban India under British rule at the time the original
was composed.

Storytelling

"There was a king" – *"Don't bother*
It was the king's footman, brother."

"His uncle, thin" – *"You sure of that? –*
Everyone knows that he is fat."

"Had a little kid billy-goat" –
"And did it a pair of wings sport?"

"One day on his rooftop, flat" –
"Flat top on tin-roofed shack?"

"In the orchard, an old gardener" –
"What gardener? It was the owner."

"Humming from a symphony, Mozart"* –
"Not Mozart! A composer upstart."

"Look, you need to *not* interrupt!" –
"Oh! Sure, ok! I'll just shut up!"

"Just then sudden jumped from bed
And came Uncle charging ahead
Caught him by a handful o' hair" –
"Where's the hair? His pate is bare!"

"So, he's bald! Why do you pout?

Good for nothing, stupid lout!

Catch you by the neck will I

And spank you hard till you cry –

Keep cutting me off mid-sentence,

Let's see where you escape hence!"

---

*The introduction of a Mozart symphony to replace the original references to Indian musical *ragas, Bihaag* and *Basant* was done mostly to assist with rhyme, and, in part, to facilitate comprehensibility for a wider audience. Other, very minor, changes have been made to aid in rhyming.

Neighbors

"Hey, heard that yesterday you said
       That the color white is, in fact, red?
(And) throughout the entire night
       Snored up a horrendous, tuneless fright?

(And) the pet cats you have at home
       Is each actually a terrible tom?
(And) this also I have heard
       Nobody at your house grows a beard?
Why is that, tell me, *ishtoopit?**
       Or will wallop ye so, ye won't forget it!"
"Quiet, you! Speak-ye-not!
       To get beaten up in anger will be your lot –"
"Make once more at me eyes vile
       Or display any aggression hostile,
Or in inimitable stupidity, avowed
       Over nothing at all, you yell so loud –"

"For threats I don't care one red cent –

Sandow's training course I underwent!"

"Jumping like a jackass again? Alright!

Come on, fight! Come on, fight!"

"The bigger they are, the harder they fall,

As you'll find out in no time at all!

If only were my uncle here,

Would beat you from here to next year –"

"Hit me, will you? Oh! Such gall –

Just you wait, let me a cop call!"

"Uh-oh! Hold on; don't be mad,

Tell me what you in mind had!"

"Of course! How silly! It's entirely true

That I'm not even really mad at you!

Why, for nothing, do we gripe?

I'm so sorry; smoke a peace-pipe?"

"Shake-hands and call me 'Brother',

Make up; go home – no more bother."

"Don't care no more – it's all alright

How do you do, and have a good night."

---

* The word *ishtoopit* is an assimilative use of the English word *stupid*, as
mangled by Bengali pronunciation. This literary device is more than 140
years old; see verse in the *Indian Charivari* (the Indian version of Punch
magazine), from 1874, mocking Bengali pronunciation of English:

"Bapre! This time you have made too beautiful picture of me,
Charivari Bahadur, *isquatting* on branch of tree;" [3]

[emphasis translator's]

That's a Problem!

Written is all in this book – world-info for novices:

Which officer's valued how much in government offices

How does one *chutney* make, how to cook *pulao;*

In great detail about elixirs and other life-hack know-how.

Soap, ink, toothpaste and such, how to make at home,

Almanacs and auspicious moments, says all in this tome.

It's all there, but on one subject advice find I none:

How to fend-off a mad bull that's charging after one!

The Daredevils

Oh! What a daredevil pair!
To the gallows headed, or prison, I despair.
One kid, ghost-like, glue-smeared face
Breaks up bottles by hitting with a slate
The other, on top of a cupboard crawls
In tantrums, from crib frequently falls.

Oh! What a daredevil pair!
Grindstones, not cornflakes, to eat up dare!
One, toothless; all with his tongue he licks,
Sits focused, sucking candles 'n matchsticks!
The other, whole rooms in blue-ink mops,
Snatches up flies, and in his mouth he pops!

Oh! What a daredevil pair!

Uncle Tom feared death to sample their fare!

He sniffed it, but suspicious, dared eat it not,

Which enraged our kid-pair, bothered and hot.

Raised hackles they; in rage, beetroot-red,

To save his hide, Uncle Tom ran away in dread.

The Delighted

Laughing we are, look at us laugh,

    laughing away so delightedly,

Three together, as one gather;

    vie each other at toothless glee.

Comes laughing my older brother,

    the younger too, and, of course, me,

No one's sure why we laugh,

    the urge to laugh find enough to be.

Think to myself, why laugh at all?

    Will eschew laughter for a while,

Even thinking that, on impulse giggle;

    crack an irrepressible smile.

With eyes open, feel the urge to laugh,

  feel it even if eyes I close,

Feel the urge within a pinch

  or a finger stuck up my nose.

Laugh at the moon, weavers' shuttles,

  even boatmen's oars in toil,

Boats, lanterns, ants and people,

  railway-trains and pots of oil.

Dissolve in laughter trying to read

  the alphabet written on a slate –

Like soda-water, bubbles laughter

  from my tummy onto my plate.

The *Ramgorur* Kid

The *Ramgorur* Kid   From laughing is forbid,
    Crack a joke, and he shakes his head,
        "Nope, of laughter I am rid!"

Always lives in fear –   Should someone laugh near
    Peers, one eye open, in cautious lookout;
        Glances here and there.

Doesn't sleep all night   With himself picks a fight
    Says, "Dare you laugh the slightest bit
        I'll wallop you tight!"

Is in a fair pickle,   The wind being so fickle,
    Won't venture out into the woods, lest
       A breeze should laughter tickle!

His mind is discontent –   As clouds moisture vent
    He's sure rumbles laughter within;
       Listens for it, intent.

Hedgerows alight   In darkness of night
    From myriad little fireflies; scared
       He is of laughter-fright.

Those who in laughter   Shake beam and rafter,
    Don't they get that it pains *Ramgorur*
       From here to hereafter?

Ramgorur's nest hidden   Where humor is bedridden
    A place bereft of fun it is:
       There laughter is forbidden.

Note: The Bengali script on the signpost in Ray's original illustration
accompanying this poem reads: *Laughter Forbidden*

Ghostly Play

Night 'fore last, without glasses, saw clear in plain sight,
Poltergeist's live ghostling – at play by moonlight.
Wriggling on his ghost-mom's lap, frolicking, exultant,
Hopping playful, thrilled and gleeful, noisy, discordant.

Heard I mom's ghostly chuckle, chortling and cackley,
Tugging his locks, checking out, her ghost-kid how lively.
Together raised giggles ghoulish of a dry ethereal mood,
Long-drawn-out rasping sighs, like saw-blade on wood.

Pummeled him and boxed his ears in mock-serious frown,
Flung him about in delighted coddle, hung upside down.

Said, "Come ye here, O my dear, precious little filthy-face,

Spread batwings; silent night with your owley smile grace.

O my dear monkey-muddle, gulpy-cuddle slimy-sludge,

Inky-forest's stinky-poodle,* my dearest porky-pudge!

O my dear rainy-summer's sunlit-hail's bandicoot,

O my dear pesky-pestle, mortar-mashed liquorice-root.

O my dear spooky kitchen's teary-titter pot-seasoning,

O my dear nightrider, moonlit gale's nightmare-ling.

O my dear stuffed-with-flour, Doughboy[†]-happy, wild boar,

Whiney-huddle, toothless treasure, cry you but once more –"

The instant she said that and slapped his face a mud-slice,

All of a sudden, trick spectral, vanished in a trip-trice![††]

---

*Ray used the term '*gondho-gokul*' which refers to a type of civet cat. In this translation 'poodle' has been used, to help with meter.

†The reference here is to the flour-stuffed Pillsbury Doughboy; not the American soldier in World War I.

††Readers complaining that '*trip*-trice' is 'invented', would be right. This translator believes that it is well within the ambit of poetic license and is certainly not too egregious an excursion. The intended meaning is *triple*-trice, signifying three times faster than a trice. This translator could have chosen to drop the 'trip' and make do with 'trice' alone, without sacrificing meaning, but chose to invent 'trip-trice' due to the obvious assistance it provides with meter.

Palm-Mystery

Nanda-Gnosai of next door, our very dear Uncle Nanda,
An affable man, very simple, no excitement on agenda.

Didn't have any ails or troubles; of worry showed no trace,
Forever appeared, hookah in hand, with a smile on his face.

Giving in to an impulse sudden, he went to see a palmist,
Came back as thin as a rake – a chattering-teeth alarmist!

Answers not when spoken to; keeps staring skywards,
Shivers frequent; eyes streaming silent tears downwards.

Came running the medicine man, and all others in wonder,
"Why do you cry? What's wrong, our dear Uncle Nanda?"

Uncle laments, "What's left to tell? Says clear on my palm,
Planet Saturn's aggravated – and my lifeline, full of alarm.

Under astral-body combos harmful, lived unaware lifelong,
Who's going to look after me, if I die sudden by evensong?

Survived some sixty years on forefathers' good deeds, past,
I'm afraid, your Uncle now might kick the bucket at last.

Can't predict, alas, when befalls what misfortunes and fears."
And so saying, and very loudly wailing, he burst into tears.

I visited him myself this morning; observed him a while –
He's a shadow of his former self; no hookah and no smile.

Sense of Essence

Mounted the king his royal throne, chimed bells the ascension
His PM's heart skipped a beat in some strange apprehension.
Demanded King, "Prime Minster, sir, why stinks your tunic?"
PM exclaimed, "Daubed essence, Your Maj;* perfume quite unique!"

King pronounced, "Odor nice or nasty, let royal physician resolve."
Claimed Physician, "I have a cold – can't in sniffing scents involve."
"Call *Ram Narayan Patro*", said King, "let him smell the stuff."
Patro pleaded, "Pardon, Majesty – my nose is full of snuff.

I've stuffed tobacco in both nostrils – can enter there a smell?"
King said, "Sheriff, then you're the one – step forward and tell."
Sheriff said, "I chewed a couple of betel leaves with camphor,
Fragrance so overpowering, my sense of smell is done for!"

King said, "Then, let us summon *Bhim Singh*, our strongman."
Said *Bhim Singh*, "I feel frightfully ill; weak, off-color and wan.
Last night I had the chills and fever – I tell you all – honest!"
So saying, collapsed on the floor and closed his eyes, soonest.

To his brother-in-law, *Chondroketu*, appealed King at last,
Said, "Maybe you could take a try, bro, pass judgement fast."
Chondro said, "If you want me killed, please call the hangman,
Martyrdom from sniffing togas, I refuse; it's more than I can!"

---

*Majesty

Nearby stood King's old treasurer – aged ninety, if not more

Thought: what harm if I have a go, am almost at death's door.

Mustered up his courage and said: "It's really straightforward,

Volunteer I, to sniff on command, and if there is a reward."

Announced King: "A thousand *rupees,** reward is yours instant!"

Up scrambled old man excited; at the prospect, exultant.

Put his nose to the PM's tunic, and in abandon, sniffed away,

Yet, stood steadfast; watched all and sundry – disbelief at bay.

Rose all kingdom in felicitation – clanged cymbal, beat drum,

What marvelous old constitution – to stench doesn't succumb!

---

*Monetary unit of British-Indian currency

The Tomcat's Song

Mystic, bare night, quietness lapped,
Plant and shrub, black velvet wrapped!
Tree-hung cobwebs tangled tight,
Fireflies twinkle a flint-struck light.
Brush, tree, sapling in silence sat,
Come, let's sing, my fellow tomcat.
Belt out fulsome tunes discordant,
Tell you which songs find I poignant.

Rises eastward at midnight's noon,
Night-blind, magenta, pale half-moon.
Reminds instant, the half-ate pancake,
I hid last night, to later a meal make.
To fetch, run pell-mell, only to see,
Licking her lips, Ol' Clip-Ear Missy!

With cheek-full pancake trying to cope;

Pouf – gets snuffed out heartfelt hope.

I question the purpose of this poor life,

Theft, sleight, larceny rampant, rife.

Unpleasant, empty, all things moot,

The missus, thunderous; face black as soot.

Pouring our sorrows into voices soulful

Come let's sing along, cat-song doleful.

Cry-Kid

Pseudo-criers cry a tawdry tune, their impact but tiny,
Nuisance wails, boo-hoo-hoo, sniveling and whiney –
Squall pitiful when hungry; sob from a good scolding,
Or if hurt all of a sudden; or of fears imagined, startling.
Smile at little, cry at little; takes but little to stop their cry:
Mothers' coddle, feeding bottle or big sisters' lullaby.

That's what I call pseudo-crying; want to hear a cry real?
Stop in your tracks, you will, awestruck; it's such a big deal.
Nondo Ghosh's next-door neighbors, Mr. & Mrs. Booth,*
Now, *their* kid is a real crier, I tell you in honest truth.

Doesn't cry every now and then; keeps bottled up his ire,
At own fancy, bawls death-inducing, to his heart's desire.
No rhyme or reason, nor whether midnight or early dawn,
Sky-shattering meaningless cry hear full of baby-brawn.

Rises cry in swelling waves, like a roaring river riptide,
Parents sit in despair, deafened; know not where to hide.
Wow! What a voice iron-clad; not a minute's recession?
Tears fall like the monsoon rain, no sign of cessation.

With rattles, dancing dolls, or a hundred sweets beguile,
Fan him or pat him down; won't get him to crack a smile.
Turns tantrum upside down, stream tears down his nose,
Bawls with mouth wide open, in 'eating-a-building' pose.
Fearsome noise, that haunted places of ghosts can rid,
Impressed to the core I am; what a phenomenal cry-kid!

Nondo Ghosh and his neighbors Mr. & Mrs. Booth are the actual names
that appear in the original Bengali. It was not entirely uncommon, in the
1920s for native Indians and the occupying British to be neighbors in
urban areas.

Fear Not

Fear not, fear not; I'm not going to hurt you,
Truth be told, at wrestling, I couldn't beat you.

My heart is too tender; my bones – ire-less,
To chew you up alive, I'm entirely powerless.

Fear you these horns that out of my head jut?
I suffer from brain ailment, I don't head-butt.

Come into my burrow; a few days here stay,
Wait on you hand and foot, will I, night and day.

My cudgel scares you; are you sure that's it?
This club is so light; it doesn't hurt one bit.

Not assured? Want me to grab you by the leg?
If I sit on your head, to be let go you'll beg!

There's me, the missus and my brood of nine sons,
Together we'll bite you. Be unafraid – at once!

Crass-Cow

Not quite the bovine, she's rather a bird, really;

Crass-cow, in *Haru's* office, anyone can see.

Heavy-lidded eyes grace an enormous profile,

Black hair well-groomed, combed in style.

Horns shaped like 'threes*'; tail, a spiral thread –

Touch her, and she moos out loud in shocked dread!

Rickety her boney frame shakes in rat-a-tat rattle,

Scold her; she falls down in a heap, all a-startle.

---

*"Horns shaped like 'threes'", in the original Bengali verse, refers to the shape
of the Bengali numeral three. The accompanying illustration here – Ray's
original – depicts the horns in the shape of the Bengali numeral.

Struggles poetry in vain, her beauty to capture,
A presence so gorgeous – just look at her picture.
She gasps and hiccups, propped against the wall,
Of whimsies unknown, oft breaks into a squall.
Charges up at times; at others, is vexed raw,
Knocked-out on occasion, suffers from lockjaw.

Eats not grass, straw, leaves or cow-fodder,
Won't mashed-gram, flour or rice-cake consider.
Likes not any meat, nor puddings vegetarian,
Only candles and soap-soup eats the contrarian.
From food of all other sort, suffers a coughing fit,
Feels nauseated and her legs shake tick-tick.

One day, a rag-strip she did, unawares, swallow,
Spent three months half-dead, head on a pillow.

If interested to buy her, any Crass-cow lover,
Will make you a good price – you think it over.

Notebook

Look, here's my pencil and here my notebook,
With writing squiggly, filled the pages look.

I write down instant as I hear new facts broach:
Leg-count of dragon fly; diets of cockroach.
Why hands that touch glue have sticky digits.
Why, when you tickle it, the barn-cow fidgets.

Observed, studied and listened to comprehend.
Wrote it all down from beginning to the end.
Why do ears ache; why a boil hurts, in turn,
Why, when it gets dark, lights one a lantern.

Ever since last night a doubt niggling, I mope –
Where put molasses – in firecrackers or soap?
The question, prompt, must I write down neatly,
For answer, I'll ask my older brother, sweetly.

Can you tell why, you get cramps with colitis?
Whence comes the bite in Aqua Ptychotis?*
Why bays the bay-leaf? Chills not chili?
Can a snore be sonorous, why livers are lily?

Whose name's Gibberish; who's Gobbledygook?
You have no answer – you haven't read my notebook.

---

*"Aqua Ptychotis" refers to the common trade name of a digestive elixir
known in popular Bengali as '*Joaaner Arok*'. The original work has
reference to that exact Bengali name. It was thought both more amusing
and convenient to use the trade name, familiar with many Bengali readers,
rather than provide a difficult-to-rhyme literal translation, such as Elixir
of *Ajwain (Ajowan)* or Bishop's Weed.

(M)address

Come, *Jagmohon!* Come, come, help me out this pickle,
Do you know where resides our *Adyanath's* uncle?
Haven't heard of *Adyanath? Khagen* you surely ken?
Shyam Bagchi is the same *Khagen's* uncle-in-law, again.
Shyam's son-in-law, *Kestomohon* – now, *his* landlord
(Whose name I've forgotten) is his uncle's brother-in-law.
His uncle's first cousin is our *Adyanath's* uncle.
Please, brother, can you get me his address in a twinkle?

Want his address? Listen up: at *Amratolla* crossing,
Three roads go three ways. Pick any, start walking.
Follow your nose straight ahead, eyes to the right,
Finally, you'll find the road curving somewhat tight.
At that point, left and right, crossroads are many,
Run circles couple, in that maze, without taking any.
Then, suddenly turn; twist out and hang a sharp right,
Left again, after three cross-streets, err not the slight.
Back you'll be at *Amratolla* crossing, once more,
Go thence wherever you will; don't bother me anymore!

Strongman

In child's-play, *Shastthicharan*, juggles elephants at random,
Weighs in at nineteen *maunds** – constitution hard as iron.

An assailant, one fine day with a bamboo staff, *Shastthi* waylaid,
Split as if were a toothpick but, as contact with his elbow it made.

The other day, walking on the street, in act of god sudden sent,
Fell from above an enormous brick, on his head by accident.
The instant it touched his head, as if were brittle sun-dried clay,
Crumbled into a pile of dust; *Shastthi,* smiling, went his way.

When *Shastthi* loudly barks, shake buildings in violent starts.

Blows if his breath too hard, in streets overturn bullock-carts.

He tears up thick wood-planks, in an instant, with a twist of arm,

Bathes in hundred barrels pond-water, sent up daily from the farm.

Mornings, his breakfast is three huge bushels pistachio nuts,

Alongside, takes fourteen pots frozen yogurt to cool his guts.

Midday, his lunch arrives in a procession of crockpots first,

Then follow nineteen jugs of iced sherbet to quench his thirst.

Afternoons, he eats nothing but four dozen sweetmeat balls,

Every evening, without fail, for stacks of fried flatbread calls.

Nightly, he gets a massage; his dozen acolytes in attendance,

With a dozen clubs they wallop loose his muscles in abundance.

If I say more, you'll think that I embellish and overstate,

Visit *Beniatola;* check it out yourself – see if I exaggerate!

Maund was the Anglicized name for a unit of measure for weight in British India, first standardized in the Bengal Presidency in 1833 as 100 Troy pounds. The measure is approximately equivalent to 82.3 avoirdupois pounds, or 37.3 kilograms. *Shastthi's* weigh of 19 *maunds* is, obviously, an exaggeration.

Learning Science

Come, let me your head examine with my hole-o-scope,[*]
See how much is adulterated and fake in your brain, dope!
Which track your brain works in, and in which is suppressed,
How much is mushy grey matter and where hollow your head.

Where goes roaming that mind of yours; why forgets things,
Which holes, so much vacuous air, into your noggin brings.
Dented head – moldy too; perhaps even cracked and nicked,
Let me analyze – sit quiet now! Why are you panicked?
Lean to a side, hold your ears, stick tongue out upside down,
I'll check you thorough, as prescribe science-books of renown.
Drop magnets into your skull, shine bamboo reflections in,
Calculate velocity using a brick, ensure your head will spin.

---

[*]The original Bengali poem calls it the *futoscope* (*futo*=hole); hence,
'hole-o-scope'.

Missed!

Oh, come see what's about to be; watch this show, magical spree
Some trickery; deceit wee; watch the birdie fall from that tree –
Thwack!

Taking up my position so, set carefully my arrow and bow
Aim upwards, shaft let go; hit your chest a mighty blow –
Whack!

On hands and knees posed absurd, *Gosttho Mama* poised on guard
To pounce on, as it falls downward; Arrow, go, fetch that bird –
Quick!

Oops! That missed by a mile; *Gosttho Mama* – you do not smile

Grazing your ribs too close, hostile; sliced arrow cut rather vile –

Nick?

Droplets

(1)

Say, man, say now, in city of Bent Bough

    Why doctors won't mashed potatoes eat?

Books demystify it, that 'tater-rice diets

    Cause brain riots; growth of intellect defeat.

(2)

Heard *Sitanath Bondyo* said quite dour?

    The sky, it seems, smells somewhat sour?

Stays not sour, though, when rain-slick –

    It's quite sweet then; taken pains to lick.

(3)

Rises rainbow in a cloud-decked sky,

    People stop to watch; let work lie.

Old man, the nit-pick, exclaims aghast:

    Gawking at that? Those colors aren't fast!

.

(4)

Drums roll boom-boom, trumpets prap-prap

    Ding-dong chimes gong, cymbals clang clap

Fearful whoop-thud-bop sounds uncouth,

    The neighbor's kid has cut his first tooth!

(5)

Listen to my story – once there was a cow,

That's where my story starts – listen up now.

Twins *Jodu* and *Bangshidhar*, best of friends,[*]

And that's where, sadly, my story ends.

(6)

Aunt O Aunt, to laugh I want

Sprouts beans on trees of *Neem* –

Elephant jolly, in mushroom brolly;

Crows' nests with stork-eggs teem.

(7)

It's a secret – to Hooghly I went

Am telling you in confidence:

There I saw three little pigs

Run hatless in exuberance.[*]

---

[*] *Droplets* has been a difficult set to translate while still maintaining the original mood, narrative and cadence. In a couple of places, a little creative liberty has been resorted to, like making the twins best of friends, and endowing the three little pigs with exuberance, for the sake of rhyme.

Muse of Whimsy

In cloudland's twilight glow,
In the half-light of a rainbow
In playful-tuned whimsies,
I trill joyful fancies.

Here forbids no constraint,
No barrier, no restraint.
Here, under skies painted,
Bob dreamboats, enchanted.

Here wells up heady music,
Bloom free blossoms cosmic,
Sense and sky tinted –
Reveal wonders unstinted.

Today, before I must go –
Say what's on my mind so;
Despite might nothing mean –
Regardless all may not glean.

I cast off, and my boat row –
Where whimsies ebb and flow.

The sprinting word who can rein?
Who today would me restrain?
In the midst today of my mind,
Beats a drum of a lively kind.

Clamors mighty issue and spew,
Words clash with words anew.
Darkness covered by the light,
So fragrant, bells peal delight.

Fancy's envoys secrets presage,
Dance the five elements on stage.
Greedy elephants hang suspended,
Their four legs in the air upended.

Rides Pegasus Grand Queen Bee,
The naughty kid; today, quiet is he.
Timeless, chill, lunar dew,
Horse-eggs bunched in bouquet new.

A drowsiness doth sleep impend –
My melodious muse is at an end.

End of Book One

BOOK TWO
Analyses & Commentary

Contents – Book Two

"Regardless all may not glean."

Introduction to the *Not* So Weird and Absurd

Let it be clear from the outset that what follows is *not* literary analysis. This translator is unschooled in literary criticism and has no pretensions to any kind of literary expertise.

The analyses and commentary focus, instead, on *investigating* the possible presence and origins of *specific dual or hidden meanings* embedded in the poems of Abol Tabol by its author. It is already well-appreciated in existing literary analyses of the work that many poems in Abol Tabol may contain covert socio-political satire.

The term socio-political has been used advisedly, as it is apparent that not all of Ray's satire was political; social commentary abounds. While hidden satire in several poems displays nationalistic overtones and targets the British colonizers of India of Ray's time, Ray has been equally impartial in poking fun at things, people and practices Indian; as well as commenting on world events. The purpose of the analyses in this book has been to unearth through amateur sleuthing which specific event, person or social practice may have been mocked or commented upon in each particular poem.

This translator relied on historical records, history books, contemporaneous newspapers and periodicals, social and political cartoons and Ray's own illustrations to conduct this investigation. The scale and scope of the sleuthing cannot be dignified with the name research. The outcomes also are quite clearly non-deterministic, even though they lead to very credible hypotheses.

Also, the quest is far from complete. It has, however, managed to uncover some very plausible connections with contemporaneous events in several poems. Some of these connections, to this translator's knowledge, have not been discovered before. Insofar that the hypotheses are plausible, they are worth sharing.

A Brief History of Abol Tabol

Sukumar Ray wrote for the children's magazine *Sandesh*, started by his father Upendrakishore in Calcutta (now Kolkata), right from the time of its first publication in 1913. At that time, Ray was living in England, where he had travelled at the end of 1911 to study photoengraving and lithography. He returned to India towards the end of 1913.

After the death of Upendrakishore in 1915, Ray became the editor of *Sandesh*, and remained so till his own untimely death in 1923. The poems in Abol Tabol, most of which first appeared in *Sandesh*, were composed during the period 1915 to 1923.[1]

Abol Tabol, meaning *The Weird and the Absurd*, was originally the name designating a section within *Sandesh* magazine where many of these poems were first published. Thirty-nine poems and seven untitled quatrains can be traced back to having first appeared in *Sandesh*.

Seven other poems making up the balance of the collection known as Abol Tabol were selected by Ray, from perhaps previously unpublished manuscripts, to form part of the final compilation.[2] Of these, Ray obviously wrote the first and last poems, both originally titled *Abol-Tabol*, specifically for the collection, possibly in 1923. Those two poems are distinguished in this translation as *Rhyme of Whimsy* and *Muse of Whimsy*, respectively.

Abol Tabol as Satire

A number of poems in Abol Tabol contain skillfully disguised socio-political satire mocking the British colonizers of India during Ray's time, as well as derision and contempt for a section of the Indian population that he saw as sycophants to their colonialist masters.

Other poems poke fun at ineffectual Indian politicians, undesirable stereotypes, social mores, value systems and customs. Ray's innate contempt for social pretensions is documented by his sister, Punyalata Chakraborty, in her book *Chhelebelar Dinguli* [Childhood

Days] (Newscript, Calcutta, 1958), in an incident where Ray rebels against being taught westernized table manners by a sophisticated aunt.[3]

Still others appear to have been composed purely in the spirit of whimsy and the humor of nonsense verse.

In order to appreciate the political messaging embedded within some of the poems, it is important to understand that Sukumar Ray was a nationalist at heart. Chandak Sengoopta, in his book *The Rays Before Satyajit* (Oxford University Press, 2016), offers evidence that "Sukumar Ray was no admirer of imperialism" by quoting an incident chronicled in *Chhelebelar Dinguli* by Ray's sister Punyalata Chakraborty, wherein Ray chides Punyalata for rejoicing at a British victory during the Boer War.[4]

Embedding hidden implied meanings of a subversive nature in nonsense rhymes for children was Ray's clever and inimitable way of subverting press censorship by the then British administration which was paranoid about seditious and subversive literature.

Supriya Goswami, in her book *Colonial India in Children's Literature* (Routledge, 2012), writes: "As the editor of a popular children's magazine, S. Ray cleverly outmaneuvered censorship practices by writing 'nonsense' for children, and had he been tried for sedition or treason for it, his trial would have ended up being as ridiculous as the trial of the Knave of Hearts in [Alice's Adventures in] Wonderland."[5]

It is a testament to the genius and creativity of Ray that not one of his poems is recognizable, on the surface, to contain any covert or ulterior message. To the uninformed reader, they read purely like delightfully humorous children's poetry which, indeed, they are.

Ray's Illustrations being as Important as his Verse
Ray drew his own illustrations for his poems, although there is evidence that he may not have conceptualized at least one – and

perhaps two – of them himself. His illustrations often disclose important clues to the inner meanings intended by him.

Ray's illustrations perfectly complement his narratives and are certainly evocative of the overt images that his verse intended to create. Hence, like Ray's verse, his illustrations too are *not* recognizable, *prima facie*, as having been simultaneously intended to illustrate his covert inner meaning as well.

However, inasmuch that they do, his illustrations must be considered integral parts of his poems: verse and picture to be taken as a whole, in order to understand them. At the time of going to press of this book, this translator considers Poushali Bhadury's excellent essay *Fantastic Beasts and How to Sketch Them: The Fabulous Bestiary of Sukumar Ray* (South Asian Review, Vol. 34, No. 1, 2013), the final word on this subject.

Previous Analysis and Breaking New Ground

This translator has provided analyses or commentary on all the poems in this book. Hopefully, they can provide glimpses of insight into the messaging therein.

A handful of these poems have been analyzed previously by scholars, and alternative explanations from the poems' overt narratives suggested. It is not the intention of this translator to repeat them in their entireties. In cases where a plausible analysis exists, the reader has been apprised of its existence, with the source acknowledged where available.

This translator has also indicated where he might disagree with existing analysis, or pointed out possible clues which, in his opinion, may have been overlooked in previous analysis.

In all other cases, the analysis is entirely new and original, or covers substantial new ground. This is particularly true about (a) references to Ray's commentary on contemporaneous events which have hitherto remained unidentified in analyses of his poems and (b) what this translator regards as 'private jokes' that, he believes, Ray embedded in his poems for his more discerning readers. Circumstantial evidence of the presence of satire regarding specific world events, and the possible existence of these private jokes has been offered in this translator's analyses of several of the poems.

The Importance of First-Publication Dates to the Analyses

It is possible to plot on a timeline, the thirty-nine poems where definite first-publication dates are known, and then compare that timeline with important socio-political events in India, and in the world, in those times. When comparing the narratives in the poems with historical events, it is possible to observe a pattern, at least for those poems that exhibit a reasonable possibility of being socio-political satire.

That pattern indicates that the first publication of Ray's commentary on contemporaneous events in the form of (well disguised) poems in *Sandesh* magazine usually lagged the event by between six and twelve months. The reasons for the lag could be manifold: firstly, even if a particular poem covertly referring to an event had been composed soon after the event, it is possible that it had had to wait its turn while other poems already submitted to *Sandesh* were being published in the sequence of their submissions. Secondly, it is also possible that Ray may have deliberately delayed the publications of some of the poems, so as to keep at arm's length the event and the commentary, in order to further obscure their connections; especially so in cases where the poems were of a nature that could be considered potentially 'seditious'.

This translator first created such an indexed timeline (reproduced on page 232) and proceeded from there to attempt to identify causal relationships between events and poems. In this he has been only partially successful, since not all poems may have been commentary, or while an event itself may have been satire-worthy, it perhaps may have been too localized, and thus escaped notice by historians.

The Need for Formal Research

This translator believes that given sufficient time and resources for thorough formal research, it may be possible to find hidden meanings in even more of Ray's poems than he has been able to uncover. In this translator's experience, where it is possible to spot causal relationships, Ray's allegorical imagery is so vivid and apt that it is sometimes possible to identify not only events and general classes of people but guess at the identities of individuals.

On Analysis being Often a Matter of Hypothesis and Opinion

The reader is cautioned, however, on two counts. First, that any new analysis presented in this volume is the product of this translator's opinion; the poems could be subject to alternative interpretations. Second, given the demonstrated lofty heights of Ray's intellect, it is entirely possible that this translator may have failed to discern hidden meaning in some poems that may, even after scrutiny, have appeared to him to be innocuous and straightforward.

Latitude in Interpretation

While analyzing Ray's poems in Abol Tabol, one must exercise self-restraint against imagining or force-fitting ulterior meaning where none might have been intended. At the same time, having examined Ray's poems, it is evident that unless Ray was poking fun at social evils or self-styled experts, he has tended, usually, to draw parallels with politically significant events. His covert narrative has always been presented as seen from his own perspective which, as far as one can discern, has always delivered an honest view of the actual ground realities of events as they applied to India and Indians.

Self-restraint has been exercised by this translator with a degree of latitude. In some of the analyses, readers may find what they might consider to be possible excursions of imagination. This is deliberate. This approach has been adopted in order to start a train of thought in the mind of the reader. Readers may choose to accept, question, investigate, augment or reject any and all hypotheses, and suggest alternative ones.

In over one hundred years since the first publications of the earliest poems in Abol Tabol, there is still not a substantial body of investigative analysis available. This translator would sooner provoke thought in order to spur fresh analysis than refrain from comment from fear of being proven wrong.

ANALYSES & COMMENTARY

Hides more in humor than just jest.
A century hasn't yet put to rest
Whether it's verse or a greater quest
For darkness that from light is wrest.

- N.R.

Rhyme of Whimsy
[Original Bengali: *Abol Tabol*]

This is the introductory poem of the collection Abol Tabol. In it, Ray offers a glimpse of things to come, as his readers, young and old alike, journey into a world of whimsy that Ray has conjured up.

Ray composed the first and last poems of Abol Tabol at the time of compiling the collection from selected poems that he had penned earlier at various times. He cleverly sandwiched the rest of the poems between these two matching bookends: the beginning and the ending poem, both titled *Abol Tabol* (distinctly titled in this translation as *Rhyme of Whimsy* and *Muse of Whimsy*, respectively).

Both the bookend poems carry embedded clues hinting that Ray had intended to leave a message for posterity about the dual nature of the poems in Abol Tabol. *Rhyme of Whimsy* is an introduction that suggests that one should expect this duality in the poems to follow. *Muse of Whimsy* (analyzed later) is a clear reaffirmation by Ray of the presence of dual messaging within the poems of Abol Tabol.

On the surface, this introductory poem seems devoid of any hidden meaning. It appears to be an innocent invitation to step into Ray's whimsical world. It promises "crazy rhymes and fun times" and a certain "wild note." It urges his readers to come carefree and mindless – and to not expect to make any sense out of what is about to follow. It exhorts them to be "Bohemian" and "Contrarian" and to challenge – "cajole and bully" – established expectations from poetry, and to nurse their "wild side" in what he refers to as "impossible, whimsy verse." Ray wrote in his preface to Abol Tabol: '*This book was conceived in the spirit of whimsy. It is not meant for those who do not enjoy that spirit.*'

However, a slightly more than cursory glance at the poem's words will reveal hidden messaging, if one is looking for it. The subtlety of this is greater in *Rhyme of Whimsy* than in its complement, *Muse of*

Whimsy, but it is there. It is a bit of a strain, at first, to believe that this poem could carry hidden meaning, but after a perusal of the analysis of its complement bookend, *Muse of Whimsy*, those doubts are likely to be largely dispelled.

Note that the crazy rhymes and fun times promised are also said to contain "drumbeats of wild note." The exact Bengali word for drum – *'maadol'* – used in the original, denotes a specific type of drum that has always been associated with war and revolution – as a percussion instrument of martial music. It is the same word that revolutionary Bengali poet Kazi Nazrul Islam would also later choose for his *Notuner Gaan* (popularly known after its first line: *Chol, Chol, Chol*), a warlike marching-song of revolution that he wrote, five years later, in 1928. "Merry mad song," in the original, is written to literally mean a mad (or obsessed) persons' song and might hint at Ray's own perhaps covertly obsessive nationalism. The adjacent verse also appears to hint at a message that if one lets one's mind go the distance, one will find meaning.

Ray invites the reader, in another meaning of his words, into a world where the mind can be without fetter or constraint, and dance to its own tune – i.e., be free to say and do what it actually thinks. He encourages the reader to be "Bohemian" and "Contrarian", i.e., to rebel and challenge the established order of things ("bully the rule-books this world's got"), and to do so in a place where the reader may nurse his or her "wild side" and be free to imagine outcomes that appear impossible today.

From that perspective, this poem is as much an invitation to join a rebellion or revolution as it is to step into a world of whimsy.

That there may be a possible nationalistic message to this poem is certainly apparent with very little stretch of imagination. However, it is only a possibility, at this time. Absent specific documented information as to Ray's intent, a possibility is what it will have to remain.

Mutant Medley

[Original Bengali: *Khichuri*]

This poem represents definite social satire about the loss of identity of the Bengali middle class – and, indeed, of much of the Indian populace – of the period. This was a period of conformity-consciousness among the educated middle class. A section of the middle class strove for conformity with the ruling British, for greater acceptance and inclusion. This often manifested itself in their affecting British mannerisms and dress that sometimes bordered on the ridiculous, like wearing a waistcoat and cap along with the Indian dhoti – with a pair of pump shoes completing the picture. Higher society gentlemen often carried walking sticks as well.

Ray's poem pokes fun at these combinations, not necessarily at dress alone, but at the very duality inherent in these and other acts of conformity. While, for most children, this might be nothing more than a funny, imaginative poem, to the informed it represented social satire. The original title translates, loosely, to the equivalent of the rather biblical mess of pottage.

The first line of this poem reads, "Was a duck; porcupine (grammar I defy)." One possible reason why this reference about defying grammar may have been included is because Ray used an unusual construct, written in Bengali as '*Hnaash chhilo; sojaru*', meaning, literally, 'There was a duck [and] porcupine' in his opening line. He omitted the conjunction and replaced it with a semicolon. It is possible, but very unlikely, that he may have done this for the sake of maintaining meter, and then felt compelled to add the justification about ignoring grammar. However, whether 'grammar I defy' was Ray's dig at the practice of ignoring one's own cultural identity and subscribing to a mishmash of duality, is anybody's guess.

Before quite exiting this subject, however, it is worth pointing out that '*Hnaash chhilo; sojaru*' is a pun on '*Haashchhilo sojaru*', which translates to '*The porcupine was laughing*'. This translator would not put it past Ray to have deliberately used the unusual construct in order to create the pun.

As noted at the beginning of this analysis, the poem is social satire. The purpose of this analysis is meant to be limited to acquainting readers with the existence of said satire. Poushali Bhadury, in her essay *Fantastic Beasts and How to Sketch Them: The Fabulous Bestiary of Sukumar Ray* (South Asian Review, 2013), does an excellent job of analyzing multiple literary aspects of that satire.[6]

Knotty Woodoo
[Original Bengali: *Katth Buro*]

This poem is probably satire on caste distinctions that played a role in the process of recruitment of Indian soldiers for the British-Indian army of World War I. Knotty Woodoo, very probably, is an individual by the name of H.H. Risley.

The original Bengali title, *Katth Buro*, translates, loosely, to 'The Old Man of Wood'. The colloquial Bengali word for wood is *katth*. The word *buro* refers to 'old man'. This poem was first published in February-March 1915.

The second half of 1914 was a period of British recruitment in India of soldiers for World War I. By the end of the war, approximately 1.3 million Indians had served. While there was good response to the recruitment calls, there was at least one issue that marred the process somewhat. The issue was the application of the 'martial races' theory to the recruiting strategy. David Omissi, in his book *The Sepoy and the Raj – The Indian Army, 1860-1940* (Macmillan Press, 1998), discusses this topic in some detail.[7]

Detailed discussion of the martial races theory and its origins would be beyond the scope of this analysis. However, in brief, according to the theory, martial races, comprising certain ethnic, religious, social groups or even castes were regarded as possessing more warlike character, greater loyalty, etc., and therefore being especially suited for military service. On the other hand, non-martial races were regarded as being unfit for fighting. This was based on cultural and racial thinking and made use of existing caste, religious and social distinctions. Physical attributes and sedentary lifestyles versus active ones might also have been factors.

The origin of the theories (there were several) is obscure. They were said to have been developed by the British after the Indian uprising of 1857. However, in later years, Herbert Hope Risley, a British ethnographer, colonial administrator and member of the Indian Civil

Service, conducted extensive studies on the tribes and castes of the Bengal Presidency. Risley formally applied the caste system to the entire Hindu population (other religions do not carry a caste burden) of British India in the 1901 census, of which he was in charge.

Risley died in 1911, but the Indian census of the same year (the one most recent to the recruitment events, since census is conducted once every 10 years) still utilized his work,[8] which was based on anthropometric data, and is, today, believed to have been based on probably unscientific sample sizes.[9] However, it shaped British recruitment policy in India during World War I.

Outside of war recruitment, it had other social consequences as well. P. Padmanabha, Registrar General of India from 1971 to 1983, in a 1978 paper titled *Indian Census and Anthropological Investigations*, writes that "… during [the] 1911 Census, particularly in Bengal, many people thought that the purpose of the census was to rank the castes rather than enumerate the people."[10]

If we stop to consider the effect of race and caste bias on the recruitment process, as well as its social effects in Bengal at that time, and allow ourselves to imagine for a moment that the various types of wood referred to in the poem represent various castes, then mocking satire does emerge about distinguishing 'martial' and 'other' races: "Which wood anemic and which is a pit-bull." The assertions about the other characteristics of woods also fit well into the martial races theories. An example would be, "Which wood gets tamed, which is peaceful;" – referring to the characteristics of loyalty and the unquestioning following of orders. The assertion that our old man knows "Which scents, for sure, with which clefts go" also appears to be a clear reference to someone (Risley) having concluded that he had catalogued potential 'martial' and other races based on characteristics that he had identified.

It is not difficult in such a case to imagine the man Risley as being caricatured as the character Knotty Woodoo: The Old Man of Wood. The old man's "charts and figures and drawn up long lists" could be a rather straightforward reference to the anthropometric measurements on which Risley's conclusions were based. The reference to the obviously impossible claim that "Sky-hung cobwebs cause knots in wood" could be a dig at the unscientific assumptions in Risley's work. The fact that it was compared to a cobweb as frail as gossamer – to use a rather circular simile – coupled with it being a pie in the sky, is also probably significant.

This translator offers no proof – only hypothesis based on circumstantial evidence – about this being a possible line of inquiry for analysis of this poem.

It is interesting to note, however, that the formal Bengali word for wood (derived from Sanskrit) is *kastthyo*. In the original Sanskrit, the 'yo' syllable is barely emphasized – i.e., spoken almost just *Kastth*. That, by remarkable coincidence, causes an acceptable pun with the word *caste*. Not exactly an unusual tool in the hands of a poet consummate with words, rhymes, puns and double-entendres. Readers are advised that we are dealing with a man who established the *Monday Club* and then often, in jest, referred to it as the *Monda Club*, making a pun with the *monda*, a type of Indian confection.

Perhaps significantly, in the actual manuscript from which Ray edited this poem for final publication, there are a couple of additional lines, one of which, when translated, reads:

> "*Katth* they *kastthyo* call – what an injustice!" [11]

This conclusively establishes that Ray had thought about the word *kastthyo* while thinking of the word *katth*.

The Old Man of Wood, translated to formal Bengali, is The Old Man of *Kastth[yo]* or – recognizing the pun – The Old Man of *Caste*, which Risley certainly was!

The Old Man of *Kastthyo*, in simpler Bengali, is The Old Man of *Katth*, and therefore, back full circle, to translate again to The Old Man of Wood – our *Katth Buro*.

Mouche Filch

[Original Bengali: *Gnof Churi*]

The Head Clerk in this poem is an interesting study in social species. Those among Bengali middle-class gentlemen who possessed slightly better than working knowledge of English were often able to obtain positions as clerks in British merchant establishments. With Calcutta (now Kolkata) being a port city with a brisk trade with England, as well as with other parts of India, Burma (now Myanmar) and Ceylon (now Sri Lanka), such establishments were many, and employed numerous clerks.

Often having risen through the ranks himself, the typical Head Clerk was a martinet, overseeing junior clerks with a lordliness rivalled perhaps only by that of a butler over footmen in large English houses of the aristocracy prior to World War I.

While this translator certainly does not intend to paint everyone with the same brush, the typical Head Clerk often did little work himself, being usually "content and tranquil at desk sit" and even "dozed in peace" while at it. His concerns, often imaginary, like a stolen moustache, had usually to be taken seriously by his subordinates, who often "ran 'round busy, in a fair tizzy" to cater to his latest whim, or risk being "fined all on the spot."

The poem also possibly takes a dig at unkind social stereotyping, rampant in those times, as when the Head Clerk seems to imply that an undesirable moustache that was "uneven cut; a broomstick but! So soiled and so grimy" could only belong to a member of what he might consider lower social strata, such as a milkman.

The moustache obviously represents a badge of authority, since it "defines the guy." The Head-Clerk appeared concerned at the daytime-nightmare-induced belief that he had lost this badge. The quality of this badge (possibly indicating rank) also appears to be important. The poem might be satire against certain positions in authority being staffed with individuals who had some means of obtaining this badge, without necessarily being qualified for it – hence, nightmares about losing it willy-nilly, too, perhaps.

While we saw in the previous poem, *Katth Buro*, that there existed a reasonable logical explanation linking it to then current historical events, this translator has been unable to unearth any clues that might point directly to there being one pertaining to this one.

However, this poem was first published in March-April 1915, which places it squarely within a cluster of poems, from *Katth Buro* to *Lorai Khyapa,* most of which have plausible connections to events relating to World War I. A niggling doubt therefore remains that there may have been a connection in this one as well.

A potential explanation may lie in the assumption that the British government may have thought it fit to temporarily curtail the powers of certain sections of the bureaucracy in the backdrop of war. If that was indeed the case, then it is possible that the Head-Clerk, who might have represented the head of a bureaucratic institution so affected, might have felt the action comparable to the loss or theft of those powers, and might be forgiven for imagining that the moustache, which represented his badge of authority, had begun to look like one that might belong to "*Shyam Babu's* milkman."

This is very probable for a couple of reasons. Firstly, given the western attire that Sukumar Ray chose to adorn the Head-Clerk with in the illustration accompanying this poem, there is a high chance that the Head-Clerk was meant to be English (Ray has, in his illustrations, almost invariably tended to use western attire to denote European personalities, and recognizably Indian attire to denote native Indians). Secondly, several times in his poems of Abol Tabol, Ray has covertly tended to use the name *Shyam* (literally meaning *black* in Bengali) to refer to the darker Indians. A disgruntled English bureaucrat complaining that his freshly curtailed powers were no better than those at the disposal of native Indian bureaucrats, deliberately lower-ranked by the British administration, is entirely plausible.

A thin potential possibility also exists that Ray might be referring to powers that a bureaucrat may have acquired through unfair means, such as paying a bribe (note: "mouche you just buy?").

Supriya Goswami, in her book *Colonial India in Children's Literature* (Routledge, 2012), provides analysis that comprehends other aspects, such as the presence, in those times, of disenchanted educated Indian professionals, the vacuous nature of bureaucratic jobs and the pettiness of inconsequential government officials. She hints at the possible presence of an equivocal message in this poem.

Prize Groom
[Original Bengali: *Satpatro*]

Prize Groom is a poem that is an absolute delight in social – and perhaps also political – satire.

Here, Ray pokes fun at the conventional wisdom in arranged marriages of that time, which often favored family antecedents of the groom over the groom's abilities, prospects, pecuniary condition and the reputations of immediate family and relatives.

Thus, a "lofty line," or in other words, a well-known lineage, which equated to higher social standing, was more important than the fact that the groom might be of undesirable appearance, poorly educated, a "deadbeat" struggling to make ends meet, and keeping poor health.

Ray takes this concept of lineage over lacunae to a sublimely ridiculous level: "*Kangsha*, the tyrant king divine" is a demi-god king in Hindu mythology who was an anti-religious tyrant of the first water. Ray implies in his satire that the lineage of even such a personage trumps his reputation, since, after all, he was a king.

Whether the poem might be possible satirical commentary on some contemporaneous appointment of an English Lord or peer to a sensitive administrative position requiring specific knowledge and ability (for which Ray may have considered the appointee unqualified), could not be determined.

Supriya Goswami, in her book *Colonial India in Children's Literature* (Routledge, 2012), also comments, in reference to the groom's nineteen tries at passing school, upon the aspect of high failure rates of natives in a biased colonial educational system.

Butting Muse

[Original Bengali: *Gaaner Gnuto*]

This poem presents a conundrum as to whether it was meant purely to be simply amusing, or if there is commentary hidden in it as well. There are a few tantalizing indications that this poem might be historical commentary, probably about an event that took place in September 1914.

In general, Ray's poems in Abol Tabol, with a few exceptions, have included veiled social or socio-political satire; especially the longer ones. From that perspective alone, there is a possibility that this one might, too. This translator has neither been able to decipher direct satire, if intended, nor uncover any previous analysis that might provide a clue. There are clues embedded within the poem, however.

The first clue is apparent when one considers the fragment "from Delhi to Burma." The reference to these two places is more than interesting. Note that *Burma* rhymes with *Sharma*. It is a fair contention that Ray had absolutely no need to resort to 'Burma' in order to produce a rhyme. All he had to do was endow Mr. *Vishmalochan Sharma* with a different last name, and Ray would have been free to choose a different word or place instead of *Burma*. It could have been coincidence, but a strong possibility exists, therefore, that the choice of Burma had been deliberate.

Delhi was associated with the seat of power of the British *Raj* in India. It had become the capital of India in 1911, predating the publication of this poem by about four years. Burma (present-day Myanmar) became a separate British colony only much later, in 1937. At the time of publication of this poem, Burma was administered as an autonomous province of British India. It is possible, if not probable, that "Delhi to Burma" was incorporated as a device to convey 'across British India'. This poem was first published in August-September 1915. Looking at historical events six to twelve months prior, the most significant event that leaps out is World War I, which commenced in July 1914.

While World War I would certainly qualify as the clamorous event described in the poem, it is not sufficiently localized to be applicable to "Delhi to Burma" only. One might turn one's attention, then, to an event relating to World War I, but localized to British India at about mid-1914 to mid-1915, which also raised a clamor and din, either figuratively or literally, or a bit of both.

From here on, it is all conjecture, but one such event that might qualify was the loud and disconcerting shelling of the Indian city of Madras by the German light cruiser SMS Emden in September 1914. According to *The Hindu* newspaper's archives, this produced an effect very similar to that described in the poem, including panic and exodus from the city, with nearly 20,000 people fleeing every day.

Until September 1914, Madras harbor was considered a safe place, secure from enemy attack. Emden had entered the Bay of Bengal on September 5, taking the British completely by surprise. Concentrating her attentions on the Calcutta-Colombo commercial shipping route, and starting near Rangoon (in Burma), Emden captured at least twenty-one ships, shelled Madras and, between September 10 and her eventual destruction on November 9, could conceivably be imagined to have caused consternation that echoed from Delhi to Burma – much like how *Vishmalochan's* singing did in the poem.

In addition to news about pervasive panic and general exodus, *The Hindu* archives also show photographs of damaged buildings and downed trees, both of which are specifically referred to in the poem.

The line "The sea-dwelling – surprising – are quiet in deep redoubt" also takes on special significance in this context if "the sea-dwelling" referred to British submarines (the E class was already in existence at that time) that, being "quiet in deep redoubt," would have been immune from the depredations of Emden. Ray might have been wondering that it was rather "surprising" that amidst the havoc unleashed by Emden, British submarines had been keeping quietly to the deep, and that Emden had not been blown-up by a torpedo from one. It is unclear, though, if any British submarines had been deployed in the Bay of Bengal at that time.

At the end of this poem, the havoc caused by the singing of *Vishmalochan Sharma* is finally ended when he is butted in the behind by a goat.

Now for a rather tenuous historical connection with a goat: Emden was eventually destroyed, her guns silenced by Australian light cruiser HMAS Sydney I, in the Battle of Cocos. HMAS Sydney had been constructed in Glasgow but was based in Western Australia. Goat Island in the Cocos (or Keeling) islands was a shipyard at that time, and a depot of the Sydney Harbor Trust. The present-day memorial of HMAS Sydney I at Bradley's point stands barely 30 minutes' drive from Goat Island.

It might appear curious that in the first line of the poem Ray wrote "summer song" when most of the action takes place between the months of September and November, until one realizes, that being located in the southern hemisphere, the Cocos islands would be experiencing summer at that time.

One last piece of fodder for thought: The Bengali title of this poem is *Gaaner Gnuto*, which, loosely translated, means 'a head-butt from song', *gaan* being the Bengali word meaning song. However, the Bengali pronunciation of *gaan* is uncannily similar to the Bengali-accented pronunciation of the English word *gun*. This translator wonders if Ray may have made a deliberate pun about SMS Emden being butted in the rear by HMAS Sydney's guns.

It must be admitted, though, that it is rather curious, and a bit improbable that Ray would portray a British victory in a congratulatory light. There are multiple alternative scenarios that may fit most of the poem's narrative. For example, the short-lived German victory against the Royal Fusiliers at the Second Battle of Ypres is a possible candidate. That would explain neither the "sea-dwelling" nor the "Delhi to Burma" localization, however.

This translator offers no proof for the above. It is simply an avenue for thought. Meanwhile, below are two images for comparison. Could the photograph on top, published in *The Hindu* in 1914, showing the damaged building and tilted lamppost, possibly have served as inspiration for the illustration Ray drew for the poem?

Photograph of the aftermath of the shelling, from the archives of *The Hindu*. Note the shape of the building, damage to its top right and the tilted lamppost, for comparison with the illustration below.

Ray's original illustration accompanying this poem in Abol Tabol.

The Contraption
[Original Bengali: *Khuror Kol*]

This poem was first published in February-March 1916, putting its date of composition probably sometime during the second half of 1915. Hence, this poem does belong in the cluster of poems that Ray has composed in the backdrop of World War I.

It is worth noting that at about this time, cartoons depicting elaborate ridiculous machines were popularized in England by William Heath Robinson (1872-1944). W. Heath Robinson began his career as a book-illustrator. Later, he also published three self-illustrated books, of which *The Adventures of Uncle Lubin (Grant Richards, London, 1902)*, is s regarded as the start of his career in the depiction of unlikely machines.

During the First World War, he drew a large number of cartoons, depicting ever-more-unlikely, complicated, ridiculous secret weapons suggested as being used by the combatants. His cartoons about World War I rapidly became extremely popular, and as early as 1915, a collection of them was published in book-form as *Some 'Frightful' War Pictures* (Duckworth, London, 1915). British servicemen took to calling any complicated piece of machinery a 'Heath Robinson Contraption'. Following its use as services slang during the First World War, the term 'Heath Robinson', denoting elaborate, complex inventions that achieved absurdly simple results, entered common parlance in England.

This poem was probably inspired by Heath Robinson's cartoons. A little more than cursory perusal of Sukumar Ray's writings is sufficient to convince one that his interests were far-reaching and his tastes eclectic. It is also known that Ray was an avid reader, not only of Indian publications but frequently procured British and American publications as well. There is evidence of the fact that he ordered those from time to time through Penrose of *Penrose Annual* fame. As the editor of a magazine catering to young readers, it is only natural that Ray would have a selected a topic that had recently captured popular imagination at the center of the British Empire and was one guaranteed to prove a subject worthy of his humor and amusing to his young readers.

Double-spread showing the fifteenth plate from Heath-Robinson's book
Some 'Frightful' War Pictures depicting a ridiculous wartime machine.
The text on the left reads:
"XV. BRITISH PATENT (applied for)
The Lancing Wheel for teaching young Lancers to lance."

However, a more sinister explanation has also been suggested by Abhik Maiti in his research article *The Nonsense World of Sukumar Roy* [recte *Ray*]: *The Influence of British Colonialism on Sukumar Roy's* [recte *Ray's*] *Nonsense Poems – With Special Reference to Abol Tabol* (International Journal of English Language, Literature and Translation Studies (IJELR), Vol. 3. Issue 2, 2016). That explanation suggests that the satirical element of the poem is that the "dangling food" represents inducements offered to Indians by their British employers:

> "... the lure of high offices and fat salaries dangled by the imperialists that produced a class of the westernized Bengalis to work for the Company till they realized that most of the high places were reserved for the colonizers themselves and not through the basis of merit."

This translator is not convinced that the above explanation holds water. The British were not known for offering promises of high-office or fat salaries to their Indian counterparts; in fact, quite the opposite. They made no secret of the fact that there existed a great divide in compensation between the British and the Indians. To wit, below is a note on bankers' salaries of the times from the book *Barons of Banking* by Bakhtiar Dadabhoy (Random House India, 2013):

> "Only Europeans could become officers and the difference in salary between them and the Indians who languished in the lower echelons was enormous. For example, the Secretary and treasurer of the Bank of Bombay was given a salary of Rs.2,000 per month while an Indian earned Rs.125 per month in the highest rank he could aspire to – that of a head clerk. An apprentice Indian clerk received no pay, but a fresh European recruit took home Rs.250 per month."[12]

Given the time of publication of this poem, the assumption that it was inspired by Heath Robinson's work appears more plausible. Whether there was additional provocation in the form of some particular contemporaneous event worthy of Ray's satire or comment, has not been possible to determine.

Battle Crazed
[Original Bengali: *Lorai Khyapa*]

This poem is very probably commentary on the heroism of Indian soldiers on the Western Front during World War I. The protagonist, *Jagai*, may very possibly be one of the few who were recipients of the Victoria Cross early in the war. In fact, in this analysis we even make an attempt to determine his identity.

At first glance, this looks like a funny poem about the crazy antics of an individual, *Jagai*, engaging in imaginary battles with imagined enemies. It has a rather poignant ending, though, in which "*Jagai* The Great expired." While the antics of the battle-crazed individual are amusing, his "dreadful [death] from sudden shot of cannon" is hardly the sort of fare one would serve up merely for children's amusement.

This poem was first published in April-May 1915, placing it within the cluster of poems inspired by events surrounding World War I. Approximately 1.3 million Indian soldiers served in the British war effort in Europe. Over 74,000 of them lost their lives. Our protagonist, *Jagai*, is probably meant to represent the Indian soldiers

In August 1914, India, as a British colony and fighting partner, sent native troops to Europe to participate in WWI. These troops were part of the British Expeditionary Force sent to Belgium. In October, they participated in the First Battle of Ypres. Our protagonist's reference to "seven Huns" ('Germans', as specifically called out in the original Bengali verse) might lend some support to the theory that this poem is about Indian soldiers on the western front. In fact, in the original manuscript from which Ray edited this poem for later publication, the word 'Germans' is mentioned not just once, but twice, in the context of enemy being fought.[13]

Shrabani Basu, in her book *For King and Another Country – Indian Soldiers on the Western Front* (Bloomsbury, 2015), provides accounts from letters and diaries of Indian soldiers on the Western Front about German shelling ("shot of cannon") faced by them, as well as descriptions of improvised explosive devices that they themselves created. The "rolled umbrella" in the poem could be referring to bayonetted rifles, and even perhaps to the improvised explosive devices and mortars that they constructed out of sections of pipe.

Ms. Basu's book also contains accounts of heroism by Indian soldiers – with three Victoria Crosses being awarded to them between October 1914 and March 1915, and eight more afterwards. It is extremely likely that news of this heroism featured prominently in Indian newspapers of the time, inspiring this poem.

If one were to hazard a guess as to the identity of *Jagai* from the events described in the poem, as well as considering the poem's first-publication date, several potential candidates emerge from Ms. Basu's book (words in italics denote rank): *Sepoy* Khudadad Khan (129th Duke of Connaught's Own Baluchis; Victoria Cross, 1914); *Jemadar* Kapur Singh (57th Rifles; (took his own life with his service pistol after facing fire from nine German battalions and fighting till his bullets ran out) Oct 31, 1914); *Havildar* Gagna Singh (57th Rifles – No. 3 Company; 2nd Class Indian Order of Merit, 1915), all in the First Battle of Ypres, Hollebeke, Belgium, 1914. *Naik* Darwan Singh Negi (1/39th Garwhal Rifles Regiment; Victoria Cross, 1914) in the Battle of Festubert, France; Gabar Singh Negi (2/39th Garwhal Rifles Regiment; posthumous Victoria Cross, 1915) in the Battle of Neuve-Chapelle, France.[14]

Of the above, Kapur Singh seems to be the most likely claimant, since, like *Jagai*, he single-handedly fought "seven Huns" (in reality nine *battalions*) and also because of the possibility that his taking of his own life is probably mirrored in the poem's last line where *Jagai* writes about his *own* death.

Today, Kapur Singh's name can be found on panel 23 of the Neuve-Chapelle Memorial at *Departement du Pas-de-Calais,* Nord-Pas-de-Calais, Neuve-Chapelle, France.

There is also a body of evidence that a number of personal journals were maintained by many members of the fighting troops, some of whom also composed poignant poetry about dying of canon fire in the battlefield. A steady stream of letters flowed from the battlefields to back home in India – after scrutiny by British censors*, of course. Wrote Shashi Tharoor in *BBC Magazine* in 2015: "The most painful experiences were those of soldiers fighting in the trenches of Europe. Letters sent by Indian soldiers in France and Belgium to their family members in their villages back home speak an evocative language of cultural dislocation and tragedy. 'The shells are pouring like rain in the monsoon,' declared one. 'The corpses cover the country, like sheaves of harvested corn,' wrote another."[15]

Jagai's "accountants' ledger tome" and his recording of his own death in it, are probably Ray's intentional references to these journals chronicling battlefield conditions and experiences.

---

* *Trivia:* Indian soldiers' letters home from the front often included messages in code to avoid redaction by censors. One such letter from Bugler Mausa Ram in the Kitchener's Indian Hospital read:

> "The state of affairs is as follows: the black pepper is finished. Now the red pepper is being used, but occasionally the black pepper proves useful. The black pepper is very pungent and the red pepper is not so strong."

'Black pepper' and 'red pepper' refer to Indian and European troops respectively.

- *The Indian Sepoy in the First World War*, article by Santanu Das, British Library WWI web project.

Caution
[Original Bengali: *Shabdhan*]

This poem was first published in November-December 1916. Here again, we have Ray poking unadulterated fun at a social species of the times: the self-styled expert dispensing unnecessary and often illogical advice regarding being mindful about personal safety and the extreme importance of exercising caution to ensure self-preservation. The advice is delivered to a hapless listener whom an expert seems to have cornered. The advice dispensed is, of course, illogical – like the possibility of being "at death's door" if one "breathed hard."

Ray, undoubtedly, discerned the potential social evil inherent in the presence, not only of such self-styled experts, but also of overly protective parents and relatives (there was no dearth of them in those times, and, perhaps, even today) who might stifle the adventurous spirit of the young by advising extreme caution in everything. The result of that would have been that the young would have been prevented from seizing initiative and adventure and miss out on opportunities and experience. Portraying such supposedly well-intentioned advice as ridiculous is an effort to encourage young readers to think for themselves by recognizing the stupidity of blindly following such advice.

Evidence of no hidden commentary could be unearthed. Underrepresentation of Bengal in the British Expeditionary Forces, doubtless caused at least partly by overprotective Bengali parents, could have been a potential trigger for this poem.

Shadow Play
[Original Bengali: *Chhayabaji*]

Shadow Play is well conceived and extremely well executed social commentary. It was first published in June-July 1916. While it is a delightfully absurd poem in itself, concerning a man who trades in shadows for a living, the social commentary against shadowy peddlers of exotic and useless remedies 'guaranteed' to cure all kinds of illnesses, is unmistakable.

Ray's times had no dearth of medicine-men and peddlers of questionable cures for all sorts of ailments, who preyed on a gullible public. Such peddlers would often display their wares on the pavement, drum up a small crowd and then mesmerize them with tales of the origins of their wares, their rarity, uniqueness, the difficulty of obtaining them and their magical efficacy, before offering them for sale at a 'bargain' price.

Ray not only captures that entire process in this poem but takes very clear digs at the uselessness of the cures and at their sole purpose being to make money for the peddler. His contempt for the practice is embodied in the original Bengali title of the poem, *Chhayabaji*, where, the word *chhaya* literally translates to shadow, reflecting the chimerical nature of the cures themselves, and also in the word *baji,* which although loosely translatable to the relatively respectable 'play', actually carries a connotation closer to the word 'trick' or 'trickery'. The entire name, therefore, conveys that the poem is about to describe a process of trickery or deceit involving something which is patently shadowy, chimerical, false or imaginary.

It is fairly simple to follow the beautifully woven sales process in the poem, starting with the intriguingly outlandish claim that the peddler wrestled with a shadow, followed by a description of the seller's extensive inventory of shadows and his unequalled prowess at obtaining the same. This is augmented by the seller expounding expertly about the behavior of shadows of trees, followed by a riveting account of how he captures them. Legitimate medicines are likened to real trees, barks, roots and saplings, and then the claim is made that compared to these "remedies futile" the peddler's home-made or 'indigenous' medications are better: "compared to actual trees, tree-shadows are better."

Where Ray gets supremely creative is where the peddler reels off, in the form of a sing-song chant, lines that sound almost like chronicled wisdom handed down through the ages:

"He who imbibes shadows of herbs, barks, roots and more,
    Good night's sleep begets he in deep sonorous snore."

These lines and several others after them read as if the peddler is reciting from wisdom inscribed in some sort of venerable encyclopedia of homely medicine. This was often a technique employed by peddlers of such remedies to provide legitimacy to their claims, and is captured with uncanny accuracy in the poem.

Ray's final blow, that the peddler's elaborate story is just a sales pitch for the sole purpose of making money for the peddler, is deftly delivered in the last line: "Priced them real cheap a vial: just fourteen *annas**." No small sum in those days.

It is possible that the reference to "completely indigenous" might also have been a dig, in part, to the *Swadeshi* (or National) movement. Chandak Sengoopta argues in *The Rays Before Satyajit* (Oxford University Press, 2016), that "Sukumar's nationalism was never blind or uncritical. When brother Subinoy got into the swing of the boycott [of British goods] movement and obtained swadeshi [i.e., indigenous – *clarification translator's*] products for use by the family, Sukumar, too, abandoned, foreign goods but in a song, teased swadeshi enthusiasts as 'a nation-crazed lot' (*dishi-paglar dol*) and indigenous products as 'unattractive, easily broken and pricey' (*dekhhte khharap, tnikbe kam, daam-ta ektu beshi*), albeit finishing

---

*Denomination of coin, of value one-sixteenth of the British Indian Rupee.

with the declaration, 'So what? They are good for the nation.' (*Ta hokna, tate desher-i mangal*)."[16]

Although the *Swadeshi* movement was first proclaimed in 1905, Mahatma Gandhi, in 1915, started the *Satyagraha* movement, which was based on the *Swadeshi* movement. This poem was first published in June-July 1916, probably in an atmosphere of renewed interest in *Swadeshi*.

One final note: Given Ray's sense of humor, it is unlikely that the number fourteen as the price, in *annas*, of the shadow-remedy is accidental. The Bengali idiom *Porey paoa chouddo anna* literally translates to: *Fourteen annas found lying on the ground*, and idiomatically means money that the finder has not had to work for.

Pumpkin-Pudge
[Original Bengali: *Kumropotash*]

The socio-political commentary in this poem against British customs and protocol is very thinly veiled and rather too obvious. Almost all commentators agree that Pumpkin-Pudge represents the British. The poem was first published in July-August 1916.

That this poem pokes fun at an authority-figure named Pumpkin-Pudge is clear. That there existed strange rules that one must follow with regard to this authority-figure's activities, is also evident.

That raises the question: which authority-figure is Pumpkin-Pudge? It has been suggested by many that Ray's satire targets the then British government in India. That could be, at a high level. Ray has written satire about British rule in several poems, including one that refers to strange laws (*The Twenty-One Law*). However, unlike in *The Twenty-One Law* where Ray's target is clearly and specifically the laws, the target of this poem isn't laws-centric, but focuses, rather, on specific strange practices that must be observed when a particular authority-figure does specific things.

Inasmuch that there is a distinction – as *practices* to be observed rather than *laws* to be obeyed, it is possible that Ray meant his satire not against government or laws, or even a functionary, but against all sorts of *protocol* (some of them doubtless mired in impractical tradition) that needed to be followed regarding the movements and activities of a functionary – perhaps the Viceroy and Governor-General of India.

It is noteworthy that in April 1916, the then Viceroy of India, Lord Hardinge, retired and was succeeded, on April 4, 1916, by Lord Chelmsford. As Viceroy, Chelmsford was invested Knight Grand Commander of the Order of the Indian Empire and Knight Grand Commander of the Order of the Star of India. Lord Hardinge had been installed Viceroy in November of 1910. Thus, it was after a period of six-years that India was witnessing a change in viceregal stewardship. It is entirely possible that the British, being sticklers for protocol, may even have published guidelines about etiquette in the presence of the Viceroy, in the days preceding his investiture.

The possibility that Chelmsford's grand titles, coupled with the possible publication of those guidelines of protocol and etiquette, may have served as inspiration for this poem cannot be ruled out.

Whether the Bengali pronunciation of Chelmsford – *Kemsphord* (the less-educated would say *Kem-so-phorod*) – may have served as phonetic inspiration for the poem's mocking Bengali title, *Kumropotash*, is anybody's guess.*

---

* If, indeed, such was the case, it would not be the first for Ray. Earlier, in open protest against the policies of Lord Curzon (Viceroy of India from 1899 to 1905), Ray had composed a poem wherein he had referred to Lord Curzon as *durjon*, meaning 'bad person' in Bengali. That time, obviously, he had the advantage of direct syllabic rhyme as well.

Note: Kumropotash is a derogatory epithet in Bengali, loosely translatable to 'fat slouch'. *Kumro* in Bengali means pumpkin; hence our translated title *Pumpkin-Pudge* – a poor cousin to the 'couch-potato'. In all fairness to Chelmsford, however – if indeed the poem had been composed to mock him – he wasn't fat at all; on the contrary, appears in photographs to have been quite fit.

Owl and Owlin
[Original Bengali: *Pnyacha aar Pnyachani*]

Little is known about the origin of this poem. No first-publication date is available. The obvious connotation in the poem is that of a mutual admiration society of two of a feather: the owl and his mate. This may hint at probable socio-political satire. Perhaps two political figures engaged in mutual appreciation in the political arena may have drawn Ray's ridicule if they had been what Ray may have considered an ineffectual pair, politically speaking.

In the context of Ms. Annie Besant's *Home Rule Movement*, the conjecture of Ray having targeted two of the three – Besant, Jawaharlal Nehru and Muhammad Ali Jinnah, does not require any great leap of imagination. (Jinnah and Nehru were not always mutual admirers, however. Also, Jinnah was thirteen years Nehru's senior, although both were political contemporaries). Moreover, Nehru and M.K. Gandhi met for the first time in 1916. Given Gandhi's propensity for a politics of appeasement of all sides, his own candidature for being one of the lampooned parties cannot be entirely dismissed either. It is, however, a matter of historical record that Gandhi and Nehru were, indeed, mutual admirers.

The waters get somewhat further muddied if one notes that in 1916, Bal Gangadhar Tilak founded the *Home Rule League* at a gathering of the Belgaon Regional Congress in Maharashtra, while Annie Besant started a second league in September of the same year, in Adair, Madras. Tilak and Besant being mutual admirers in the political arena (especially with one of them male and the other female) holds possibility that they may have been represented in the poem as the owl and his mate.

Another, less obvious, pair of candidates comprises Panchcowri Banerji, editor of the Calcutta newspaper, *Nayak,* and the Anglo-Indian press (essentially the English-owned press) in Bengal. Banerji and the Anglo-Indian press, at that time, had appeared to be agreeing on their views regarding an incident that rocked Presidency College, Calcutta and much of Bengal in 1916.

In February 1916, there occurred an assault by some Indian students on one Prof. Edward Oaten of Presidency College. Details are irrelevant to this analysis, but the Anglo-Indian press blamed the students. Reaction in the native press was mixed: while a section was simply uncomfortable with the idea of the students having had taken matters best left to the law into their own hands, others, including *Nayak*, were openly critical of the students. Satadru Sen, in his book *Disciplined Natives – Race, Freedom and Confinement in Colonial India* (Primus Books, New Delhi, 2012), writes: "Panchcowri Banerji, editor of *Nayak*, saw the assault as evidence of a growing cowardice and viciousness among students... Panchcowri – who, it has been suggested, was a police informer – spelled out the reasons for the decline into behavior that was both unmanly and unyouthful [*sic*]. 'Two causes are gradually spoiling our boys', he wrote, 'and they are commercialism in education and so-called patriotism."[17]

Quite apart from the question as to who had been at fault in the incident, it could be surmised even then, perhaps, that the students had had provocation for the assault. Knowing what we know today about Ray's own covert nationalism, Panchcowri's remark about 'so-called patriotism' is unlikely to have gone down well with Ray.

This translator suspects that deriving phonetic inspiration from Panchcowri's first-name, Ray referred to him derogatorily, in pun, as the *Pnyacha* (Owl), with the Anglo-Indian press being the *Pnyachani* – mutual admirers in their condemnation of the Indian students.

No direct correlation between the year 1916 and the probable period of composition of this poem can be made, however, because this is one of those poems where the date of first publication is not known.

As an irrelevant aside, among the students involved in the assault – and one of two expelled – was one S.C. Bose, who, in 1943, led the revival of the Indian National Army.

Tickling Old-Timer
[Original Bengali: *Katukutu Buro*]

Tickling Old-Timer is a well-known character in Abol Tabol. Whenever Ray has introduced a character, it has usually been either as a thinly veiled reference to a real-life character Ray intended to lampoon, or as personification of a type of character or practice that Ray intended to provide satirical social commentary on. While this may not necessarily be true for all of Ray's characters and poems, the overwhelming evidence in most of his other poems points to the probability that the same may be true in this case as well.

It is frustrating, however, absent any contemporaneous reference or later analysis, to try and guess at what Ray's intent may have been. It has often been possible, given the history of the times and recognizable references in Ray's poems, to draw conclusions that have an air of logical respectability, a certain possibility and high probability. No such recognizable reference leaps out from this poem. There are only embedded clues that one has to go by. Perhaps they might provide enough food for thought for an historian familiar with Ray's times, to suggest an explanation. The poem was first published in May-June 1915.

The first source of clues comes from the original illustration accompanying the poem. Sometimes, conclusions can be drawn about Ray's intent from the original illustrations, since Ray drew them himself. The first thing to notice would be the attires of Tickling Old-Timer and his victim. Old-Timer's clothes are decidedly western, while that of his victim are the *dhoti* and *kurta* (known as *dhuti* and *panjabi* in Bengali) of a middle-class Bengali gentleman.

The relative sizes of Old-Timer and his victim, unfortunately, generate more questions than answers. Old-Timer has been drawn as much bigger than his victim. This does not necessarily indicate that his victim is a child. The victim is dressed more like an adult than a child of those times, especially with regard to the length and drape of his dhoti. (Confusingly, the only indication that the drawing might represent a boy rather than a man, is the lack of facial hair; but that is inconclusive). The victim also deports an air of docile resignation. So, was Old-Timer meant to represent the ruling British, as a class, bigger (in political power) than the natives, or would that be reading too much into it?

Moreover, it does not help that Old-Timer's shoes are not contemporary British at all, but look rather elfin, like something Puck might wear in *A Midsummer Night's Dream*. Does that make Old-Timer a 'fictitious' character, or in other words, non-existent – a figment of imagination?

The second source of clues is, of course, the poem itself. Unlike other poems where Ray has poked fun at the colonialist power, its laws and its protocols, where the natives were at the receiving end without recourse, in this poem there appears to be a choice of avoidance: "...go you will wherever, / Of Tickling Old-Timer, beware, *avoid him* forever." It appears that sufferance is no longer the badge of the ruled, but that there might be an actual possibility of them avoiding the source likely to cause the suffering. This does not seem descriptive of the prevailing perceived relationship between the British rulers and their Indians subjects at that time. Chances are high, therefore, that Ray's target is *not* the British colonizers as a ruling class. Or, at least, Old-Timer does not represent them.

Most curious is that "No one's sure where he lives; across which streets." If one does not know where Old-Timer lives, why, then, does one need to be warned to "never at home visit" him? Surely, he is not to be found?

As to what might happen if one wandered, unawares, into Old-Timer's home, the analogy in the poem is quite straightforward. One must listen to supposedly humorous, but, in reality meaningless, stories, and then laugh at the supposed humor. This seems to be pointing towards some sort of *indoctrination* where one must agree with a set of dogma or doctrine being presented through supposed example or parable.

Successful indoctrination is parodied as succeeding in making one laugh. Since there exists the certain peril of being made to laugh by being tickled with a feather, it appears that Old-Timer will not shy away from resorting to torture to achieve that indoctrination. It also appears that the benign feather-torture is applied in combination with the indoctrination by default, and that towards the end, one even runs the risk of being poked and scraped in the ribs and pinched in the nape!

So, what does one have here? A warning to stay away from a torturing indoctrinator of silly (or perhaps seditious) ideas, who cannot be found and may be fictitious?

That opens up a whole new line of thought. Was Ray's satire, if any, then directed not at an individual or class, but at some actual warning that might have been issued by some authority – quite obviously the British – to the general populace, exhorting them to avoid someone, somebody or something?

It is not inconceivable that true to their habit of issuing wartime propaganda posters, the British might have also felt compelled to issue propaganda warning native Indians to steer clear of insiders, perhaps not entirely imagined, who might be preaching sedition.

The possibility of Ray having ridiculed such propaganda as scaremongering about an imagined peril that had no basis in reality – here, the 'fictious' Old Timer to be avoided – is completely in tune with the nature of the rest of his writings, both in Abol Tabol and beyond.

Derelict Shack

[Original Bengali: *Burir baari*]

The analysis of this poem might prove to be difficult. It is simple to theorize that it is social commentary on the plight of Bengali widows of the times, who often led a sort of semi-ostracized existence from mainstream society, very often in penury. This was less prevalent among the educated but was rife among the lower middle class and in the villages – especially for widows with little or absent any means of sustenance.

An alternative explanation has also been suggested by Abhik Maiti that the house loosely held together is, in fact, a portrait of the colonies; the old lady being meant to signify Queen Victoria herself and the gradually failing attempt of the colonizers to maintain the colonies in the aftermath of the First World War, when mass revolution had already begun to foment in several colonized geographies.[18] This reference appears anachronistic, since the reigning monarch at the time was George V, but is still a pretty plausible explanation.

The poem was first published in December-January 1918.

The Quack
[Original Bengali: *Hatourey*]

First published in August-September 1916, this poem is very probably social commentary on young British members of the Indian Civil Service (ICS), thoroughly unprepared to manage the responsibilities that they were tasked with.

Hatourey, loosely translatable literally as *The Hammerer*, is an idiomatic Bengali term used to describe quacks, i.e., doctors and medicine-men of little or no formal learning in the medicinal arts, who yet declare themselves physicians. Over time, its ambit has expanded to also include doctors with actual formal training, but with a reputation for not really understanding their field and prescribing treatment after treatment in the hope that one will work.

This practice, akin to a mechanic using a hammer to hunt for faults by sounding a non-working piece of machinery or in the hope of jolting a jammed mechanism into working, is where the epithet, Hammerer, comes from. The word for hammer in Bengali is *hatouree*. The idiomatic English translation of the word *hatourey* in Bengali, as applied to members of the medical profession, is the English word *quack*.

The poem appears, on the surface, to be simply a hilarious depiction of a wannabe doctor, with an ending play of words between the idiomatic hammerer and the literal hammer. In socio-political commentary, it probably refers to young British recruits in the Indian Civil Service (ICS). The implied satire very much might be that these administrators had no clue what they were doing and had a one-size-fits-all approach to all problems.

This was far from unusual; on the contrary, rather the norm. Shashi Tharoor, in his essay *The Un-Indian Civil Service* (Open magazine, August 12, 2016), writes: "The British system of rule in India was, by any standards, remarkable. A 24-year-old district officer found himself in charge of 4,000 square miles and a million people. He was subject to the tyranny of the 'Warrant of Precedence'..."

Tharoor probably meant to say simply 'precedent'. In clarification, he quotes H Fielding-Hall, who in 1895, after 30 years of service in the ICS, wrote: "The whole attitude of Government to the people it governs is vitiated. There is a want of knowledge and understanding. In place of it are fixed opinions based usually on prejudice or on faulty observation, or on circumstances which have changed, and they are never corrected. Young secretaries read up back circulars, and repeat their errors indefinitely... 'following precedent'."

These back circulars were probably the "paper-dolls first for practice" in the poem. Small wonder, then, that "Cholera or dengue, the cure is the same."

Notes: (1) Indians had started appearing for the ICS examinations since 1860. Racial discrimination was pervasive, however, with multiple instances of Indians being passed over for promotions or dismissed for minor infractions.[19] English officers still made up the majority in 1916, when this poem was first published.

(2) *Warrant of Precedence* (sometimes referred to as the Blue-Book) was an actual physical reference-booklet detailing precedence in order of rank – from Viceroy to the lowest-ranking ICS officer. It had nothing to do with the concept of following precedent. In using the phrase 'tyranny of the warrant of precedence' in an idiomatic sense, Tharoor got across the point about being a slave to precedent correctly, but the *Warrant of Precedence* is a totally inappropriate and incorrect example.

Wacky No-One
[Original Bengali: *Kimbhoot*]

The Bengali word *Kimbhoot*, can be translated into English to mean strange, weird or wacky, usually implying at the same time a jumble or hodge-podge. Hence, a "weird jumble."

This is a delightful poem with lessons for young readers. Our protagonist in the poem is not content with the features and attributes he is endowed with but craves and covets the endowments of his animal and bird brethren, for reasons of acquiring 'desirable' attributes that would supposedly make him better.

In implied warning to his young readers about being careful about what they wish for, Ray depicts the plight of our protagonist when his wishes do magically come true. Not only is our protagonist in danger of being ostracized in the animal kingdom, he also ends up suffering from an identity-crisis.

Multiple instances of credible analysis exist that here, once again in social commentary, Ray laments the loss of identity of the Bengali upper middle-class who embraced many practices of the British ruling class in an attempt to appear more anglicized than their neighbors.

This poem was first published in September-October 1918.

To Catch a Thief

[Original Bengali: *Chor Dhora*]

This is an amusing poem in its narrative, and it is hard to tell if there was any social or socio-political commentary that Ray had intended, although that is not improbable at all.

Whether or not there is a message hidden in this poem may be difficult to tell only from its words. However, as this translator has pointed out before, Ray used to draw his own illustrations for his poems. Sometimes, clues to what Ray may have been thinking can be gleaned by careful observation of those illustrations.

Unfortunately, we can only gather certain pointers from Ray's illustrations that perhaps can set us thinking in suggested directions. After that, lacking further corroborative evidence, it is a matter of guesswork at best, but still, it is fun to consider clues that may be present in Ray's illustrations.

In Ray's drawing, our protagonist is waiting with sword drawn to bring his wrath down upon the culprits who have been stealing his food. The important things to notice are the following: one, our protagonist is looking in the opposite direction while his food is being stolen from behind, and two, the thieves are not people, as he imagines, but birds and cats.

Is there a message inherent in the picture? Is Ray pointing to some contemporaneous event wherein the person or entity being robbed, or otherwise affected, has no clue as to who or what is robbing him, and is not even aware in which quarter to look to find the culprits? Is he subscribing to some sort of conspiracy theory in his mind, in which he thinks that the culprits are a group or faction (symbolized by the imagined people), when there might be a far less sinister explanation (symbolized by the birds and cats)? It would be hard to tell without a study of contemporaneous events, and even then, one could probably only speculate and conjecture.

This poem was first published in *Sandesh* magazine in March-April 1918. As a perhaps irrelevant aside, the poem's narrative, if augmented by the illustration that birds and cats were stealing someone's lunch while the person thought it was humans doing so, bears uncanny resemblance to a children's short story, titled *Detective*, that Ray also wrote for *Sandesh* in October-November 1917, i.e., six months prior to the publication of this poem. This translator has read that story in the original Bengali. It appears that the prose version, at least, was written purely for children's enjoyment, with no ulterior meaning intended. However, it may have been repurposed in the poem for social or political commentary.

It's All Good

[Original Bengali: *Bhalo re Bhalo*]

This poem is curiously nonsensical, though not in literal meaning, but perhaps because it seems to be begging a *raison d'etre*. It is hard to imagine an ulterior motive to this poem than pure whimsy.

As with many poems in Abol Tabol, lack of serious research into contemporaneous events prevents us from speculating if there had been anything implied beyond the mere words.

It is an interesting flight of fancy, though, to conjecture if Ray was mocking a political entity or a member of the media who might have been taking a conciliatory line to some series of contemporaneous happenings, adopting a culture of appeasement. i.e., "all is good."

In such a case, one might imagine that Ray's contempt for the entity is delivered in the last line: "pancake and maple syrup" implying that this entity lacks the imagination and vision beyond the pedestrian and mundane.

This poem was first published in May-June 1923.

What a Surprise!
[Original Bengali: *Awbaak Kando*]

This poem's message is a simple one. Here, Ray gently suggests to his young readers that supposedly awe-inspiring personalities may, indeed, be mere mortals like other everyday people.

In this poem Ray attributes certain rumored normal daily activities to a druid (a literal translation of the original Bengali word would be closer to medicine-man). Ray talks about these attributes in the form of questions designed to indicate that people perhaps may have thought differently about the druid prior to those rumors having surfaced, and they may have believed him to have been someone special or magical.

Except for the first line, every line of this poem ends with a question mark. The questions are posed in a manner indicative of the fact that they are, in fact, rhetorical, asked in jest, and do not require a response. The poem concludes with an implied message to not necessarily accept widespread beliefs, but to verify them first.

In his own quirky humorous fashion, Ray manages to turn the messaging on its head, and does not suggest that any rumored special or magical attributes of the medicine-man be checked out by his readers, but rather that his readers verify if the rumors concerning the druid being normal like everyone else might be true. Nevertheless, the moral is to not blindly accept tales that may simply turn out to be the result of popular imagination, but to check them out for oneself.

Whether the poem targets any recognizable particular entity of the times (perhaps a Surgeon-General) who might have been publicly portrayed as grand or awe-inspiring, is unknown. The work was first published in October-November 1922.

Babu – The Snake-Charmer
[Original Bengali: *Baburam Shapurey*]

Previous analyses have graced this short poem with multiple interpretations, several of them far-fetched. They tend to vary from relating the events that led to this poem to ancient history, set in the year 1717, to events in contemporaneous times, i.e., 1920s, as told through the eyes of British colonizers.[20] This translator finds neither scenario compelling. There have also been suggestions that Ray may have targeted Indian political entities or organizations.

The latter suggestion is far more probable – that Ray was referring to the political climate of the times and pointing to ineffectual native Indian entities, either in politics or perhaps in journalistic quarters, whose token opposition to the British could be likened to harmless snakes in the poem: the type with no 'nails' and horns and those that do not hiss, bite or fight. One such individual could easily have been Mahatma Gandhi, who in those times advocated non-cooperation with the British government through non-violence and peaceful resistance.

There is more than one reference within the poem that Ray may, in fact, have had two individuals in mind ("put up two snakes" and "bring me a couple"). If so, this translator is unable to venture a guess as to who the other might have been. If the targets were not individuals, Ray could have been referring to both the Congress Party and the Muslim League, the two main Indian political organizations of the time – both of which Ray may have considered ineffectual.

It is worth noting that these were times when the British government had started to make a token attempt at involving native Indians in political governance. Their influence continued to be limited, however, and it is quite probable that Ray may have likened Indian political figures to puppets dancing to the tunes of the British; Babu, the snake-charmer representing none other than the British government.

It is amusing to note that British cartoonists in England in the 1920s had ideas similar to Ray's when it came to mocking the behavior of the British government in India. Reproduced on this page is a photograph of page 235 from *Punch Magazine* of London, dated March 5, 1924, less than three years after the first publication of this poem in June-July 1921. An original page from the magazine, authenticated by J. Sewell of London, forms part of a private collection of this translator.

Photograph of page from Punch magazine, March 5, 1924.
Photographed from the original in the translator's private collection.

In it, British cartoonist Leonard Raven-Hill makes fun of an almost identical subject with nearly identical caricature. Here, a snake named *Swaraj* must perforce be 'charmed' by the British Secretary of State for India, whether it 'like[s] it or not'. *Swaraj,* meaning self-rule, was the name of a movement for demand of the same, by the Indians, from the British.

The dialog in the cartoon, titled *No Change of Air*, goes like this:

> The Snake: "I had hoped for something more congenial from this new instrument [*labelled 'Labor Government' in the image*]."

> The Secretary for India: "The instrument may be new, but I don't propose to change the tune just yet. Meanwhile you've got to be charmed with it, whether you like it or not."

Ray's contempt for what he may have considered ineffectual Indian political leadership can be summed up in the actual literal translation of the last line of the poem, wherein the narrator expresses a desire to cause physical harm to the snakes; at the very least, "knock 'em out cold" with a stout stick.

King of *Bombagarh*
[Original Bengali: *Bombagarer Raja*]

This poem is a bit of a puzzler. The narrative in the poem is about the outlandish customs practiced in the fictitious kingdom of *Bombagarh*. Supriya Goswami, in her book *Colonial India in Children's Literature* (Routledge, 2012), provides a very plausible analysis.

This poem was first published in October-November 1922 and belongs in the cluster of poems that include *Babu – The Snake-Charmer, Crass Cow* and *The Twenty-One Law*, the three which immediately preceded it in their order of first-publication dates. Just as we can see that earlier, in 1915, Ray had composed a cluster of poems about events relating to World War I, we can observe somewhat similarly in this 1921-22 cluster, a common theme of mocking Indian politicians under British rule, Indians aping British manners and customs, and also, satire on British laws for India.

The puzzlement stems from the fact that there is a wealth of detail provided in the poem in the form of allegory. Also, we have often observed that Ray usually tended to comment on a specific contemporaneous event or practice. At the very least, his poems appear to have been triggered by them. Nothing specific springs to mind in this case, indicating, possibly, that this poem may be a candidate for further research.

Ray rarely ever used a word without reason. It is, therefore, reasonable to suppose that each line in the poem probably refers to some specific silliness. It is difficult to determine what exactly each line ridiculed, but one can make guesses. However, this translator has found it hard to express an opinion for all lines. It may be safe to assume that the pillow on the queen's head refers to elaborate coiffures that ladies wore in their hair, and that red-rouge paint refers to face makeup.

Experts (Ray used the word '*ostaad*' which can translate to either 'musician' or 'expert') with heads and necks covered in quilts, very likely refer to ceremonial headdresses and elaborate collars and lapels of multi-folded fabric. Contemporaneous illustrations show, for example, legal experts dressed in similar fashion. Postage stamps on heads of pundits seem strangely evocative of the square mortarboards worn on the head by academicians. Fried mango wafers in photo frames could very well be referring to yellowed parchment of royal decrees, marquees or citations of honor received from the British or even maps displayed by the 'king' – perhaps the ruler of an Indian princely state.

It has been suggested that enclosing fried mango wafers in "boundaries" represents the redrawn borders of Bengal in 1905.[21] This translator is unable to agree with this suggestion. Firstly, because there is absolutely no deployment of the word 'border' or 'boundary' in the original Bengali of this line, and, secondly, because it turns out that the reference to 'borders' actually first appeared in a 1987 *English translation* of this poem which went like this: "Have you heard of the monarch of Bombagarh's orders / To fry mango jelly and frame it in borders?"[22] It is this translator's opinion that 'orders' and 'borders' were chosen in that translation primarily for the sake of rhyme, and also that that particular translation is not quite as literally true to the original words as it could have been. He will concede, however, that a fried mango wafer in a photo-frame could have represented a map of Bengal.

Could nails hammered in loaves of bread refer to sandwiches for high tea, held together with food skewers? Not entirely improbable.

It has been suggested that the king yapping at audience signifies that only the ruler had freedom of speech. It has also been suggested that the cricket-playing aunt and the dancing uncle signify how the ruling class took scant interest in affairs of state but spent their time in idle western pursuits.[23] Perhaps.

However, it is entirely reasonable to ask why the descriptions of the outlandish activities presented in the poem are presented in the form of questions. Observant readers will remember that in a previous poem, *What a Surprise!* all but the first line ended with question marks. It is exactly the same for this poem, *King of Bombagarh*, as well. In the previous poem it was simple to see that the questions were rhetorical, asked in jest, and did not require a response. It appears that the same literary device may have been employed by the poet in this poem as well.

If the questions are asked in jest, let us ponder a moment, *not* on the individual questions themselves, but what they might collectively represent. What does dipping an expensive precision instrument, such as a pocket watch, in lard signify? What does making one's bed with sandpaper mean?

Is it possible that the collective weirdness involving the mango wafers in photo-frames, nails in loaves of bread, watch, sandpaper, the playing of cricket with pumpkins and the broken bottles hung from the throne was meant to signify ridiculous uses for objects meant for other functions?

This translator is reminded of an alleged* incident, that took place in the 1920s, involving the Maharajah Jai Singh of Alwar, relating to the *deliberate*, ridiculous use of an object meant for a different purpose.

Amrit Dhillon in *Bejewelled Carriageways* (The Telegraph, U.K., 2004), recounts that one day, the Maharajah, looking nondescript and almost shabby, walked into a London Mayfair car showroom, interested in a Rolls-Royce Phantom II Tourer. A young salesman snubbed him, convinced that the man was wasting his time. The Maharajah bought all seven cars in the showroom and had them shipped to India, with the salesman as escort.

When the gleaming cars with beaming salesman arrived, Jai Singh apparently appeared briefly for a perfunctory inspection, ordered that the cars be used for collecting municipal garbage forthwith, and continued to employ them for this purpose till Rolls-Royce wised up to the bad publicity and apologized.[24]

Do the broken bottles hanging from the throne represent garbage being collected by a Rolls-Royce Phantom?

It is certainly possible that the king's mistreatment of a revered example of engineering such as a Rolls did not sit well with the technologist that Ray also was (see brief biography on page 245).

Perhaps one might pause to ponder why, despite all the weird things happening in the *land* of Bombagarh, the title of the poem is still *King of Bombagarh*. Why is *that*, "can someone tell me?"

---

* This translator was initially unsure how much of this story is fact, and if portions may be apocryphal. However, *The Telegraph, U.K.*, did run this story in October 2004, quoting corroborating evidence from the Maharajah's descendants.

Note: Several other versions of the story can be found on the internet, some complete with pictures of one of the alleged cars, with brooms tied to its front-bumper. The reader is cautioned, however, that that picture appears to be that of a 1934 Ford Tudor Sedan, and, therefore, is unlikely to be authentic.

Word-fancy-*boughoom!*
[Original Bengali: *Shobdokolpodroom!*]

Ray's original Bengali title for this poem, *Shobdokolpodroom!* is a word that he coined. *Shobdo* in Bengali means 'sound'. It also means 'word'. *Kolpo* is an abbreviation of *kolpona*, meaning imagination, and *droom*, adopted in Bengali from Sanskrit, means tree or bough.

Kolpodroom also has a specific meaning of its own in the Bengali language: it means a 'wishing-tree' or a tree that grants wishes (better recognized in Western cultures as the wishing-well) – wishes being anything that one might imagine or fancy (*kolpona*).

First published in September-October 1920, this poem is a signature creation by a consummate manipulator of words. It relies primarily on the figure of speech called the onomatopoeia, which means a word that – in pronunciation – phonetically imitates, resembles or suggests the sound that it describes. Words like 'bang', 'boom', 'clink', 'whoosh' and 'thud' all belong in this category.

Where Ray really displays his genius is when he combines onomatopoeia with idiom to create humor. An example will make this clear: For instance, in Bengali, the word for 'drown' or 'submerge' is commonly idiomatically used in the context of the sun and moon to indicate the setting of these astral bodies. Ray skillfully evokes onomatopoeic words for drowning such a "glub, glub, gloop" to describe a setting moon, thus linking idiom with onomatopoeia.

This serves to elicit a chuckling response as the reader appreciates how silly a 'drowning' moon might sound if taken literally, but how perfectly acceptable it is in established idiomatic usage.

Numerous creative liberties have been taken with this translation, the reason being that when translating from one language to another, it is extremely improbable that the same onomatopoeic words would relate to the same idioms in both languages. For example, in Bengali, *raat kaate* idiomatically means "the night is spent," but the literal meanings of *raat* and *kaate* are 'night' and 'cuts' (verb), respectively.

Ray was able to use onomatopoeic words that describe the sounds of cutting or sawing and relate them to *raat kaate*. This translator did not have the same luxury, since the 'night' does not 'cut' in English, but, rather, is 'spent'. This translator has, therefore, resorted to the "clink" of coins and related it to the night being spent – like coins or loose change.

Overall, however, the translation preserves the onomatopoeic connection with idiom for all of Ray's lines, even if it changes the literal meaning of the event or idiom that Ray originally intended. For example, "Puff-Puff! Pant-Pant!" has been used as onomatopoeic stand-ins for the act of running, to relate the literal act with the idiomatic expression: "the colors *run*," i.e., the colors of the blossom aren't fast but tend to get washed away. (In the original, Ray wasn't referring to colors, but to the scent of the blossom evaporating.)

"It's the falling dew; please mind your head!", on the other hand, by a stroke of coincidental luck, is both literally and idiomatically true to what Ray intended.

Sometimes, a compromise has been reached between literal translation and intent. In Bengali, the process of waking up is idiomatically called *ghoom-bhanga* (literally, *sleep-break*). Ray used onomatopoeic words for sounds of breakage to link them with the idiomatic sleep-*break*. This translator, prevented from using the words sleep-break (since, unlike *break*fast, sleep-break is not normal English), uses the words 'wake-up' and links them to the onomatopoeic 'whoosh' as the sound of 'wake' going 'up' by rocket-ship.

Appreciation of Ray's true genius with this poem would be incomplete without a brief analysis of the poem's title. It is clear that in this poem Ray has played with sounds and words (both called *shobdo* in Bengali). It is equally clear that this play has been influenced by flights of Ray's fancy (*kolpona*). The word *droom!* with the exclamation mark, may be considered an onomatopoeic word for explosion (and, indeed, is often used as such in Bengali).

So, Ray's coined title, *Shobdokolpodroom!* denotes an explosion of words and sounds, fueled by fancy. At the same time, it is a *kolpodroom* of *shobdo*, or wishing-tree of words, that provides gifts of fanciful humor for the reader. Such was the genius of the man.

It is unknown if this poem is satire against what Ray may have considered equivocation by the British administration, whose proclamations may have been either at odds with practice or could have held simultaneous alternative interpretations – as in the poem. The hint of *bombast* in the explosion of words and sounds could also be pointing towards mocking satire in such a context.

Given that this was a period in time when the British administration in India was making public proclamations of involving more Indians in government, it is not inconceivable that Ray may also have compared the imaginary nature of a wish-granting tree (*kolpodroom*) to what he may have considered the false – and hence, imaginary or dubious – nature of proclamations and promises made by the British administration, which, in words borrowed from Shakespeare, were "full of sound and fury, Signifying nothing."

Once Bitten Twice Shy
[Original Bengali: *Nera Beltolaay Jaay Kobaar?*]

One can analyze the lines in this poem to discern potential satire against the presence of the British government in India in Ray's times.

First published in November-December 1918, this is the longest poem in Abol Tabol, with a story told almost in the style of a ballad. It is also the one with the longest title. It has a somewhat more complex rhyming scheme than most other poems in this collection. The poem can be broken up into four-line stanzas, wherein the first three lines rhyme with each other but the fourth or last line in a stanza rhymes with the fourth or last line of the following stanza. That rhyming scheme, known as the Violette, has been preserved in the translation.

This translator has been unable to unearth any direct references to whether the poem may have specifically meant anything beyond its overt narrative, but, speaking in generalities, the poem offers at least three clues that raise several questions and, if nothing else, hint at a hidden message.

First, there is the king, whom we shall suppose as being a wise monarch – since there is later indication in the poem that he was dear to his subjects – who sits in the hot sun wearing a warm woolen jerkin. His response to his discomfort is not to take his jerkin off, but to call for rain and blocks of ice to cool himself. This does not sound very wise, which leads one to wonder whether there is a foolish-king parable hiding somewhere in Ray's intent.

Second, while the reader is told that the king is writing on his slate things that no one can understand, we later discover that his preoccupation is neither particularly kingly nor concerning matters of state. Instead, the king seems more worried about a hypothetical character, and the number of times this character may be shy of some activity once he has had a bad experience (been bitten) in the performance of it – but, amusingly, stemming from a foolish *literal* rather than the proper idiomatic interpretation of the saying *Once bitten twice shy.*

Third, towards the end of the poem, the answer to the kingly dilemma is provided not by learned experts or pundits, but by a mere child (note: in the original Bengali it was a humble water-carrier instead of a child). Furthermore, the answer continues to treat the king's ridiculous, foolish literal interpretation of the saying *Once bitten twice shy* seriously, replying in the literal context as well.

The absurdly humorous part, of course, is that the king seems to be interpreting 'being shy of' not in the idiomatic sense of 'avoiding' but in a sense as if 'being shy of' is an activity that one proactively performs at will – and, indeed, may be at the risk of performing over and over again countless times, unless checked, or induced by some means to desist! The absurdity of the king's thought process is a clear message that the king is perhaps not only foolish, but also is burdened with imaginary concerns of no consequence to his subjects or to the process of governance.

There are several unanswered questions right from the outset. For example, why does the king take his seat on a pile of sunburnt bricks? Why does he wear a woolen jerkin in the heat? Why does he feed from a bag of peanuts yet does not swallow them?

It has been well-established that several poems in Abol Tabol contain Ray's skillfully hidden contempt for the then British rulers of India. The following is, of course, speculation on the part of this translator, but, does the "ruddy-face[d]" king represent the British Crown? Is the symbolism of the king taking a seat on a pile of sunburnt bricks simply indicative of the British Crown's presence in hot and sunburnt India?

Is the king's propensity for continuing to wear a woolen jerkin in the heat indicative of the British *Raj* clinging steadfastly to the ways and customs of England, with scant regard for their relevance to India and to the integration of the British with the natives whom they governed?

Is eating from the rather proletariat bag of peanuts symbolic of an outward show of trying to fit in with Indian subjects, while, not actually swallowing the nuts betrays the fact that this is only a put-on act?

Is the king's command to his subjects to "get a downpour in" to be interpreted to mean that the *Raj* felt all-powerful – as if it could command nature? Is the preoccupation with trivial and absurd problems indicative of the lack of will to tackle issues of a real governance of benevolence?

Given Ray's penchant for taking veiled pot-shots at the British, these are all valid questions. This translator, however, readily admits that the questions stem merely from educated guesswork, and in the end, are still questions only, and that he has no answers.

Explanations

[Original Bengali: *Bujhiye Bola*]

This is a brilliantly funny poem about a self-styled 'knowledgeable' person's frustrations in trying to impart knowledge to the "young these days" with their "impatient ways." He corners his hapless young victim, *Shyamadas*, into "[sitting] here a moment" so that he might explain a "thing vital" to him.

Poking fun at a social stereotype: the local self-styled font of wisdom, Ray takes us through an entertaining journey as this gentleman more-or-less fishes his 'student' out from important daily chores, in order that his victim might "comprehend sans fail" whatever "useful stuff" our protagonist is attempting to "insert" into his brain.

The story is all the funnier when we realize that this is an oft-repeated occurrence, and that our protagonist is simply starting over from where he left off from the time "when last [they] aligned."

That the "knowledge" being imparted is absolute nonsense, is masterfully conveyed by the gobbledygook bombast that he sprouts about "orbs of matter" that "from fine to coarse transform" and its improbable connection with a "sunlit grass-patch" and a "moonbeam-sliver juxtaposed to match."

Our protagonist, of course, fails in his quest, as *Shyamadas* is bored to the point of yawning, and finally gets up and leaves in disgust, calling whatever that was being taught "just stuff and nonsense."

It is possible that this poem, unlike many others in this collection, has no hidden message, other than the very straightforward one of warning Ray's young readers of the existence of personalities like our protagonist, their characteristics, and that it is ok to avoid them. All the while enjoying a brilliant piece of humorous poetry, of course!

Converse to the thesis on the previous page, there is a faint outside chance of this poem having been a disguised, sarcastic lament on the lack of interest among then Indian students in scientific education.

Given that in Ray's illustration accompanying this poem *Shyamadas* and the person who is trying to impart knowledge to him are both dressed in Indian garb, it is a reasonable supposition that both entities are Indian. Clearly, neither is British, since attire worn (western versus Indian) is a device that Ray has almost always employed in his illustrations to distinguish the two. Therefore, it is unlikely that the British or their colonial education system may have been targeted in the poem; it appears that this is purely domestic commentary involving only domestic actors. In this thesis, the younger protagonist represents the "wayward" Indian youth while the elder one the well-intentioned Indian educators of the times.

While the elder (and presumably wiser) educator may have been genuinely interested in imparting useful knowledge, the subjects taught may have seemed gobbledygook and "stuff and nonsense" to his audience. What those subjects may have been is skillfully hinted at by Ray. "Orbs of matter" that "transform" and produce "thrust" at the "root of the five elements" refer, likely, to physics and chemistry. Sap collecting in the roots of a bough may possibly be referring to the subject of botany. The symbolism of the rest is difficult to guess at, although it must be admitted that a "chimerical" bough does appear somewhat philosophical – which does not fit our thesis well.

Ray was a graduate of physics and chemistry himself and is credited with internationally acknowledged contributions to photography and printing technology. Contemporaneous youths' preference for working with the "thesaurus" – perhaps signifying language and the softer arts – could have goaded him to compose this as a sarcastic poem. Overall, however, the earlier thesis appears more plausible.

This poem was first-published in January-February 1919.

Hookah-Face *Hyangla*
[Original Bengali: *Hnuko Mukho Hyangla*]

While this poem offers several clues that it is socio-political commentary, it also leaves some unanswered questions, the chief among them being, who is Hookah-Face *Hyangla?* We can work out that he represents the conformist portion of the Indian population intent on aping all things British. The poem was first published in March-April 1917.

In the poem, going by Ray's own original illustration that accompanied it, Hookah-Face *Hyangla* is a sort of animal with elephantine legs and two tails. So, if this poem is, indeed, social commentary, he obviously represents some contemporaneous entity with certain overt characteristics. It is also possible to guess, because of later developments in the poem, that this entity probably represents a stereotypical individual common in those times. We can even build a postulate that he represents a class of Indian subjects under British rule who blindly aped the British – but more on that later in this analysis.

What is not clear are the reasons behind the choice of name for the entity: Hookah-Face *Hyangla,* and his place of abode, *Bangla* or Bengal. *Hnuko Mukho Hyangla*, the original Bengali title of the poem, translates loosely to *Hookah-Face Hyangla*; the hookah being an instrument for smoking tobacco. *Hyangla* means wretchedly greedy (usually in the matter of food). It could also be translated into the modern connotation of the term 'needy' where the implication is of one who is whiney-needy rather than so in a pecuniary sense.

One question is, what does Hookah-Face mean? Someone with a face shaped like (the bottom end of) a hookah, or someone who is always seen with a hookah held up to his face? Another question is, why is this entity wretchedly greedy or wretchedly needy? Finally, did Ray mean to restrict this entity's place of abode to *Bangla* (Bengal), or was *Bangla* chosen to rhyme with *Hyangla*? Obviously, the reverse could also have been true – i.e., *Hyangla* was chosen to rhyme with

Bangla (in which case, restriction of place of residence is the correct theory), which only complicates matters further.

This translator has chosen to adopt the notion that Bangla was chosen to rhyme with *Hyangla*. Therefore, the assumption is that the entity Hookah-Face represents a class of Indian subjects under British rule, not necessarily restricted to the province of Bengal.

Now we venture into uncharted territory, but this translator urges the reader, after having considered the arguments that follow, to assess whether the proposed thesis is feasible.

In the original Bengali, Hookah-Face's uncle *Shyamadas*, the "drug-cop top brass" is described as *'aafimer thanadaar'* or literally, 'police inspector in charge of opium'. The phrase could also mean 'caretaker of opium' or 'storekeeper of opium'. In fact, Ray's original manuscript from which he edited this poem, says *'aafimer dhamadaar*[25]*'*, which translates to 'the person in charge of the basket of opium', or idiomatically, 'peddler of opium'.

If we ascribe this position, somehow entrusted with the control and/or distribution of said narcotic, to be a metaphor for the ruling British (not an unreasonable excursion of fancy, since the *thanadaar* or police inspector position represents authority), and we take into account that a hookah can be used to smoke opium equally as expeditiously as tobacco, we can build our postulate that Hookah-Face is not hookah-faced with regard to the shape of his visage; rather, is always seen with a hookah held to his face because he is constantly smoking, out of a hookah, the opium (read 'cool-aid' or propaganda of mannerisms, way of life, etc.) doled out by his indulgent 'uncle', the British.

The word for uncle used in the original Bengali verse is the one that specifically means *maternal* uncle. In Bengali culture, maternal uncles are traditionally considered to be indulgent towards and protectionist of their nephews. The ruling British as indulgent and protectionist towards their native supporters would tend to make a lot of sense in this context.

A picture then begins to emerge, of a class of natives drunk on British propaganda, unable to think for themselves and, to use a very modern-day American expression, fat, dumb and happy to dance to the tune of the British ("Thump-thump plump feet / He used to dance beat") on not too agile, elephantine feet. Not forgetting that this class of native is also *Hyangla* or wretchedly needy for more of what it craves to ape.

However, what about the theory of aping itself? Fortunately, the poem offers clear evidence on that score.

First, a brief history-lesson in Bengali humor: In the original Bengali version, the phrase "This strategy to swat flies" is written as *'maachhi mara fondi ae'*. This can be literally translated to mean 'this is a fly-swatting strategy' (with the sense of cunning or trickery heavily implied in how the word 'strategy' is used here).

The humorous connection is as follows: In the days of no photocopiers and scarce carbon paper, a bevy of clerks was employed to make exact copies, called true-copies, of important documents, by hand. The apocryphal story goes that a certain clerk, while copying an important document, came across a dead fly squashed between its pages. Not knowing how to make a true-copy of that, he reportedly swatted a fly that he found conveniently buzzing around and stuck its carcass in his copy in the exact spot as in the original. The legend of the *maachhi-mara kerani* – literally, fly-swatting clerk – was thus born. Hookah-Face's admission that his is a fly-swatting strategy, is clear evidence that he is referring to himself as being a copycat.

Not one to stop at merely pointing out the existence of this cool-aid-drinking, wretchedly needy, fat, dumb and happy copycat native indulged by the British, Ray takes the poem to further heights of humor, delivering more scathing messages in the process. Since the entire strategy of existence of members of this class of native is based upon copying their colonialist masters, the natives know how to do only what they have seen done before or have been told to perform by their masters in some prescribed manner. So, as analogy in the poem, should a fly sit to their left, they know to whack it with their left tail. Should it sit right, they whack it with the other one. However, in the process of blindly aping others, this class has lost the ability to think for itself. Therefore, when faced with the unfamiliar situation of a fly sitting in the middle, it "can think not what to do." It has no recourse: it has "no more tail but two!"

Priyadarshini Bhattacharyya, in her essay *Tracing the 'Sense' behind 'Nonsense': A comparative study of selected texts of Sukumar Ray and Edward Lear* (International Journal of English Language, Literature and Humanities, Volume II, Issue X, February, 2015), provides a short analysis with similar conclusions.

In addition to writing brilliantly humorous poetry skillfully disguised to be totally unrecognizable as the seditious or colonialist-mocking literature that it was, Ray often embedded in his poems private jokes for his more discerning readers. Such an example can be found in this poem in the choice of the name *Shyamadas* for the (British-representing) uncle. The word *Shyam*, literally translated, means the color black. The word *Das*, literally translated, means servant. What better joke than to refer to the British as *Shyam-a-das* or black-servant – the exact opposite of the white masters that they were? The choice of name, and hence the private joke, was very probably deliberate.* However, it is also possible that Ray may simply have been referring to a native Indian person working as a *daroga* or lower-level police inspector in charge of a *thana* or police station (hence, *thanadaar*) – a fairly common occurrence in the British-Indian local law-enforcement apparatus. This latter idea is less probable, though, due to the presence of the 'indulgent maternal-uncle' reference discussed earlier.

---

*For readers curious about the regularly accepted *non-literal* meaning of the name *Shyamadas*, it means Servant of God – the god, *Krishna* in the Hindu pantheon being also named *Shyam* because of his dark complexion.

The Twenty-One Law
[Original Bengali: *Ekushey Aeen*]

This poem, as pointed out by Supriya Goswami, in her book *Colonial India in Children's Literature* (Routledge, 2012), quite obviously ridicules unsavory laws laid down by the British for their Indian subjects.

These were turbulent times in British-ruled India, with the Rowlatt act having been steamrolled through India's Imperial Legislative Council by the British in 1919, despite unanimous opposition from all Indian quarters.

Among other things, the Rowlatt Act sought to maintain many provisions of the Defense of India Act of 1915 that included many sweeping powers for the British administration, including summary arrest without warrant, vaguely worded laws (with wide latitude of interpretation) about sedition and seditious writing, and potential summary imprisonment without due process.

The laws were extremely unpopular and led to many protests and violent incidents across the country. Finally, under widespread pressure, and accepting a report of the Repressive Laws Committee, the Government of India repealed the Rowlatt Act, the Press Act, and twenty-two other laws in March 1922.

Ekushey Aeen, meaning *The Twenty-One Law*, or alternatively, The Laws of Twenty-One, was first published in August-September 1922.

It is unclear if Ray intended 'twenty-one' to mean the year that had just gone before the repeal of the Act or whether 'twenty-one' has some other implication. After all, the Rowlatt Act had been in effect from 1919 to 1922. This translator is wary of labelling anything that Ray wrote as coincidental, but, of course, coincidence is a possibility as well, although perhaps not a very probable one. It is, however, possible that 'twenty-one' refers to the day and year of the visit of the Prince of Wales to India (he landed at Bombay in November 21, 1921). The day of his arrival was marked by general strikes in India, called at the behest of Mahatma Gandhi. Also, 1921 was the year in which the British administration promulgated an ordinance outlawing the *Volunteer Brigade* of the Congress party. Noted Bengali author Narayan Sanyal, in his book *Kholamone* (Deys Publishing, Kolkata), surmises in Bengali, "... the travails of November 21, 1921 led Sukumar Ray to compose *The Twenty-One Law.*" *

It is unclear which particular law was being targeted in each of the six stanzas of the poem. It appears reasonable that the first and last stanzas refer, respectively, to the possibilities that one could accidentally and involuntarily fall afoul of these laws.

The second and third stanzas, similarly, probably point towards laws relating to unreasonable requirements for licenses for certain activities, and unreasonable taxation, respectively.

The fourth stanza seems to be parodying an environment of reduced or straightjacketed freedom, wherein one could be penalized for deviating from the straight and narrow for as ridiculous an offense as looking "left and right" instead of straight ahead while going about one's business.

However, the fifth stanza about "people who poetry write" getting "locked up in cages tight" unmistakably refers to the laws about summary arrest and seizure of persons and equipment suspected of being involved in seditious writing.

In his signature style of humor, more often than not containing some private joke, Ray refers to such suspected writers of seditious literature as people who write poetry; knowing full-well, of course, that he himself quite frequently engaged in what might be considered seditious – or, at the very least, anti-British – writing, skillfully disguised as delightfully humorous poetry for children.

---

*The existence of this opinion from Sanyal was brought to the notice if this translator by Alaka Mukherjee of Chandannagar, West Bengal, India, which assistance he acknowledges with thanks.

Ding-a-ling and Dong
[Original Bengali: *Dnaare, Dnaare, Droom*]

This poem was first published in June-July 1917.

It is long enough of a poem to have hidden meaning embedded, but, unfortunately, nothing exactly leaps out at this translator. On the surface, it is a poem about the importance of taking time off to relax and let one's guard down occasionally in a life otherwise full of chaotic bustle, problems, work to be done and seriousness in general. Several metaphors, like chaotic traffic, streets filled with mud after monsoon rains, and piled up office work are invoked to represent the above.

A bunch of musicians who "staunch[ly] endeavor to drum a delightful song" perhaps serves as the metaphor for our inner muse that, inside all of us "thrums [in] a beckoning beat." The chance of this being the case is very slim, though; Ray wasn't much given to waxing lyrical.

In literal meaning, the poem urges its readers that it is "better if [they] dare, to toss all care" and "sing along" with their inner muse. In that exhortation, the poem is strangely evocative of the introductory poem in the compilation Abol Tabol, which calls upon Ray's readers to "come mindless, be boundless" and to "lose [themselves] in impossible, whimsy verse." This poem may, therefore, contain similar messaging about marching to the "beckoning beat" of revolution.

While the above analysis may perhaps be acceptable from a literary standpoint, considering that Ray wasn't much given to waxing lyrical, it is possible that this poem has some hidden meaning. Some additional clues might be gleaned from Ray's illustration accompanying the poem. The illustration is far from straightforward, however, and raises several questions. The first clue in the illustration is, of course, the attire worn by the musicians. One of them is dressed in European jacket and trousers, implying that he is either European or, perhaps, even a native Indian conforming to western style. This gentleman also sports a very distinctive moustache and has back-brushed hair. Are those details intended to convey a personality that was perhaps recognizable at the time of composition of this poem? Who might he be? He seems to be reading the lyrics of the song from a piece of paper he holds in his hand. What might be the meaning of that? Of the other three people depicted in the illustration, two are clad in dhotis, indicating that they are probably native Indians. The gentleman standing behind the person clad in European attire has a definite feline cast to his face, and, to boot, sports what looks like three medals on his chest. Is he perhaps, then, Sir Ashutosh Mukhopadhyaya (anglicized Mookerjee), – also known as the *Tiger of Bengal*? It is difficult to tell from the illustration if he is also sporting Sir Ashutosh's distinctive moustache, but the distinctive shawl is very much in evidence. The other dhoti-clad personage is sitting. Why is that when everyone else is standing? The remaining gentleman playing the cymbals is bald. Why so? Also, what exactly is he wearing, and what might that attire mean? Why is he much smaller in stature compared to the others? Why are these people, collectively, the musicians? What ties them together?

Furthermore, all the above gentlemen appear to be placed on a sort of carpet, whose four-corner-reinforced design seems to indicate that it was intended to depict a 'blotter', a very common desk-accessory in those days of inkwell-dipped pens. Does that mean that there is an implication of a bureaucratic scenario wherein a bureaucrat is 'at play', with the characters depicted as puppets?

Illustration at this level of detail points strongly towards the poem having been intended to convey social or political satire, perhaps even targeting some particular incident. Unfortunately, it has not been possible to decipher what that might be. Perhaps a reader with detailed knowledge of history of the times might be able to offer an explanation based on the clues described above.

Storytelling
[Original Bengali: *Golpo Bola*]

This is an amusing poem very reminiscent of a theme often found in children's literature, the latest and most modern example probably being a sub-theme in *Diary of a Wimpy Kid* by American author Jeff Kenny. The age-old favorite theme here is that of a not-so-bright older brother attempting to sound off as knowledgeable and sophisticated to a younger sibling but being thwarted by the sibling's superior knowledge in the process.

In this poem, the older brother starts off by saying "There was a king..." and is immediately cut off in mid-sentence – "Don't bother..." – by his younger brother, who, in fact, appears to have better information: "... It was the king's footman, brother."

This goes on for several new topics started by the older brother, with the younger invariably getting the better of him till the older is so incensed that he promises to "spank [his younger sibling] hard."

The similarity with the frequent interplay between Greg Heffley and his older brother Roderick in *Diary of a Wimpy Kid* is unmistakable. *Diary of a Wimpy Kid* is but a modern example. The theme, obviously, is not, and has always been one possible to milk for the amusement of young readers.

Whether the poem was meant to be purely amusing, or Ray meant to lampoon a pair (possibly of politicians), as was his wont, appears lost to history. No first-publication date is known, either.

Neighbors
[Original Bengali: *Narod! Narod!*]

This poem invites analysis on several levels but is probably political commentary involving the Congress and the Muslim League – the two dominant Indian political parties of the time.

Firstly, however, the poem is as an opera glass looking back into the times. It offers fascinating views of some interesting usages of English words and phrases adopted into the Bengali language. It also provides some historical insight into fitness and bodybuilding products marketed to the general public in those days.

As satire against social-stereotypes, it pokes fun at quarreling neighbors – antagonists, perhaps since antiquity; a fixture, doubtless, in all ages and times.

With respect to the adoption of English words into Bengali, this poem demonstrates two fascinating examples of assimilation across languages. The word *ishtoopit* as used in this translation (as also used phonetically in the original Bengali verse) is an assimilative use of the English word 'stupid' as adopted into Bengali pronunciation. This translator has left it virtually unchanged from the original. "Speak ye not!", as used in the translation, written in the original Bengali as '*speak-ti not!*', translates literally to 'do not [do the act of] speak[ing]', or idiomatically, to 'shut up!'

The reference to "Sandow's training course" is to Eugen Sandow (born Friedrich Wilhelm Müller; 1867-1925), who was a pioneering German bodybuilder, credited as being the father of modern bodybuilding. Sandow authored a book titled *Strength and How to Obtain It* and was also the creator of *Sandow's System of Physical Training*. This poem was first published in 1917, eight years prior to Sandow's death, and doubtless, proves that his body-building system (this translator substituted the word 'course' for 'system', in order to reduce a syllable and preserve meter) was popular in those times. As an irrelevant aside, Sandow is also apocryphally credited with having popularized the men's undergarment 'singlet', still known in some parts of the world as the Sandow vest.

From the standpoint of poking fun at social stereotypes, one has only to look at the obviously outlandish and patently trivial accusation that one neighbor levels at the other: "you said, that the color white is, in fact, red" and "the pet cats you have at home, is each actually a terrible tom," in order to realize that mockery of the quarreling neighbor stereotype could have been Ray's overt intent.

Secondly, analyzing this poem symbolically, this duo of quarreling neighbors, and the fact that they make up in the end, coupled with the timing of first publication of this poem, September-October 1917, provides important clues to the potential political satire that might also be covertly present in the poem.

In 1916, the Indian National Congress and the Muslim League, the two main political parties in India, who did not see eye to eye with each other on multiple issues, came to an agreement and established cordial relations at a joint session held in the city of Lucknow. It is more than probable that this poem is political commentary on the disagreements between and eventual – temporary – reconciliation of these two political parties.

Significantly, Ray's original illustration for this poem shows one neighbor wearing the sacred thread of a Brahmin – conclusive evidence that he is Hindu. His opponent is drawn sporting a goatee. While that is not conclusive, it is significant that the goatee was a form of beard most popular among Muslims (and avoided by Hindus – who did not wish to be mistaken for Muslims) in those times. Recall that "nobody at [their] house grows a beard."

Ray never ceases to surprise us, however, with his simultaneous multi-level thinking and the hidden private joke that is present in many of his poems. Looking back at the mocking of social stereotypes and the seemingly outlandish and trivial accusations that the neighbors were hurling at each other, we can perhaps be forgiven if we initially neglected to suspect that the color white might stand for the more moderate or the 'soft faction' (known in those times as *'naram dal'* – a literal translation) of the Congress party, led by Gopal Krishna Gokhale, and the color red for the 'hot faction' or *'garam dal'*, led by Bal Gangadhar Tilak.

With the presence of two factions within Congress with such diametrically opposed philosophies, perhaps the Muslim League could be justified in questioning the Congress if their overtly peaceful (white) stance was, in fact, covertly militant (red). The symbolism of ostensibly pet cats who are actually "Terrible-tom[s]" in reality, could easily be referring to covert militants in the guise of peaceful party workers.

That's a Problem!
[Original Bengali: *Ki Mushkil!*]

It appears that just as Ray has poked fun at self-styled know-it-alls in other poems, he may have done the same in this poem, but, instead of at a person, at an encyclopedia. Of course, by extension, that might also apply to the know-it-all(s) who may have contributed to the encyclopedia's volumes.

The narrative clearly questions the usefulness, to the lay person, of the knowledge presented in the book, and suggests that while there are many facts chronicled within its pages, it seems to be wanting in the ability to dispense practical advice. Whether the book in question is something as famous as the Encyclopedia Britannica or some other less famous volume is anybody's guess.

This poem was first-published in January-February 1918. There *does* appear to be something going on with the Encyclopedia Britannica right about that time. The eleventh edition of Britannica had been published in 1910, and it had been a best-seller. The war years, however, had not been kind to its circulation. Consequently, the future of Britannica had been at stake. It was rescued from certain bankruptcy when philanthropist Julius Rosenwald, the CEO of Sears Roebuck, bought its rights in February 1920.

This translator is not aware if there were any discussions in the Indian press about Britannica's future during the period 1917-1918 that might have inspired Ray to comment, but it is a fact that Britannica was well-known in India in those times. See top-right of the image on the previous page, of an advertisement of Britannica that appeared in *National Geographic* magazine in the USA in February 1913.

The poem could also have been about some other, more localized, almanac or gazette. It being about a government gazette is a strong possibility since "which officer's valued how much in government offices" might be indicating towards government pay-scale schedules published therein.

The Daredevils
[Original Bengali: *Daanpitey*]

Far-fetched as it may sound, this poem probably contains commentary on the reaction of the United States to The Treaty of Versailles, signed in June 1919.

Or, it could be something entirely different. It depends on whether 'Uncle Tom' in the poem is meant to signify the British or the Americans. Supriya Goswami, in *Colonial India in Children's Literature* (Routledge 2012), provides an alternative analysis unrelated to the Treaty, based on the former assumption.[26] This translator does not necessarily disagree with the line of that analysis. This alternative explanation is being provided as another potential avenue of inquiry.

First, however, one needs to answer the question why Ray would be interested in the Treaty of Versailles at all. It turns out that the signing of The Treaty of Versailles was important news in India and, also, specifically in Bengal. The reasons being that H.H. Ganga Singh, Maharajah of [the Indian Princely State of] Bikaner, along with Edwin Montagu, the then British Secretary of State for India, also signed the treaty on behalf of India. The Bengali lawyer and politician, Satyendra Prasanno Sinha, or Lord Sinha as he is better known, was also present but excused himself from signing, preferring to remain on the sidelines, describing himself as "just a foot-soldier of reform."[27]

Now, why might 'Uncle Tom' be American rather than British?

It has been suggested by Sukanta Chaudhuri that that the daredevil kids described in this poem have been inspired by *The Katzenjammer Kids*, an American comic strip created by the German immigrant Rudolph Dirks in 1897.[28] Information about *The Katzenjammer Kids* and a later derivative, *The Captain and the Kids*, is fairly easy to come by.

In this comic strip, the frequent victim of the hell-raising kids was 'The Captain'. Ray's illustration that accompanies this poem, of the kids and the old bearded gentleman, is significantly similar to the portrayals of the Kids and The Captain in the strip. It is probable that Ray found the images appropriate and – well – appropriated them, with modifications, for his poem.

Ray calls the old man 'Uncle Tom'. This seems more indicative of referring to America than Britain, for the following reasons:

Ray has usually tended to use the epithet *Mama* or maternal-uncle to signify the British (see poems *Hookah-Face Hyangla, Neighbors* and *Missed!*). Referring to 'Uncle Tom' in the original Bengali verse, he specifically uses 'Tom *Chacha*'. *Chacha* is an unmistakably *paternal*-uncle reference. Why the deviation from the usual in this case? Perhaps a distinction from the British was necessary?

Note also that the U.S. was already known as Uncle Sam as far back as 1812.[29] American novelist Harriet Beecher Stowe's *Uncle Tom's Cabin* had been published in 1852. *The Katzenjammer Kids* is an American comic strip. Ray's use of *Tom*, even though the universally recognizable *John* Bull to signify the British was available, is also probably significant. (True, the British *Tommy* did exist, but he was a much younger soldier and certainly no 'Uncle').

Based upon the assumption that Uncle Tom signifies the Americans, the following is the thesis:

The Daredevils was first published in August-September 1919. The actual signing of The Treaty of Versailles occurred on 28th June 1919, but it had been in negotiations ever since the end of World War I. Towards the end of the negotiations, the main conditions of the treaty were determined at personal meetings among the leaders of the 'Big Three' nations: British Prime Minister David Lloyd George, French Premier Georges Clemenceau and American President Woodrow Wilson.

Wilson had been vested in the process from some time ago, with what was known as his Fourteen Points, which, among other things, focused on rebuilding the European economy.

Clemenceau, on the other hand, was hell-bent on ensuring crippling financial reparations to be made by Germany, and on securing territory for France. Lloyd George, too, supported reparations, but to a lesser extent than Clemenceau. By the time *The Daredevils* may have been composed, it was becoming clear that Wilson was not in favor of the high-handed terms against the Germans in the treaty.

Wilson, Lloyd George and especially Clemenceau were often at loggerheads regarding the terms of the treaty. Recall that in the poem Uncle Tom was wary of eating the kid's food: "Uncle Tom feared death to sample their fare." Whether Uncle Tom represents Wilson, with the kids representing Clemenceau and Lloyd George, we shall never know for sure, but a possibility exists that the kids' fare which The Captain refused to sample may have been referring to the treaty in its then current form at the time *The Daredevils* was composed.

Note also that Wilson did, or would have "feared death" at a political level in connection with this treaty which was inextricably linked with the idea of America joining The League of Nations. Ben Walsh, in his book *GCSE Modern World History* (John Murray, London 1996), cites several reasons why Americans were opposed to being signatories: (a) German immigrants in America being against the harsh terms to Germany, (b) cost, (c) isolationism and (d) dislike of old empires, being among the foremost. The treaty was going to cost Wilson his reelection.

This translator has not been able to make a guess as to the meanings of all the symbolic activities of the kids described in the poem, but at least one reference can be connected to the French demand for territory. That one kid "whole rooms in blue-ink mops, / Snatches up flies, and in his mouth he pops" could be indicative, based on the color blue, of France intending to redraw the map of Europe with substantially more French territory. It is not inconceivable that the act of snatching up flies and popping them in the mouth is a dig at this land grab. Among other things, Germany lost all her colonies: "the Allies had shared them out like thieves dividing the swag."[30]

SYKES, in *Philadelphia Evening Ledger*

"Stop that, both of you."

Cartoon by Charles H. Sykes in the Philadelphia Evening Ledger.

Coincidentally, the imagery of the kids and the old man, conveyed in Ray's verse and augmented by his illustration, is somewhat similar to an early World War I cartoon by Charles H. Sykes, published in the *Philadelphia Evening Ledger*, and later reproduced in *Cartoons* Magazine, where the kids are England and Germany, and the old man, the United States.[31]

Whether Ray had ever seen this cartoon and drawn inspiration from it is unknown, but it *is* known that Ray was quite familiar with American periodicals, and there is evidence[32] that he ordered some from time to time through the British establishment Penrose of *Penrose Annual* fame.

The Delighted
[Original Bengali: *Ahlaadi*]

This poem is probably about what is historically known as 'assertive nationalism' in India, and three Indian statesmen, known popularly together as Lal-Bal-Pal.

The poem was first published in February-March 1919, putting its date of composition anywhere from then backwards to perhaps six months earlier. Some of the analysis of this poem will probably forever reside in the realms of conjecture, but it is worth an attempt.

This poem, when combined with the illustration that originally accompanied it, is unique in one aspect: this is the only poem where significant evidence is available that although the illustration for it may have been (re)drawn by Ray, it may not have been an original conception.

Firstly, unlike most of Ray's other illustrations, this one is unsigned. Secondly, it appears to be an exact copy of an illustration drawn by William Wallace Denslow for Lyman Frank Baum's book *The Wonderful Wizard of Oz* (George M. Hill Company, Chicago, 1900), to depict a group of fictitious people, referred to in the book as the Hammer-Heads. Denslow drew these creatures without arms. He also drew three of them, dressed identically, but with slight differences in the bowties that they wore. The illustration accompanying Ray's poem mirrors both these attributes.

Ray was a prolific illustrator of his own poems. Certainly, it is more than evident that he had no particular need to borrow someone else's illustrations. Yet, he deliberately chose to adopt what he must have considered an extremely apt illustration from a book likely to be already well-known among the well-read of his day. Ray, as was his wont, was probably once again embedding his own private joke for his more discerning readers. This translator has chosen to proceed with this analysis based on that assumption.

It is well-known that *The Wonderful Wizard of Oz*, although a children's novel, was in fact political allegory, even though Baum never offered any conclusive evidence that this was intentional. In that respect, Baum and Ray are certainly very much alike. Baum's work had been influenced by the Brothers Grimm, Hans Christian Andersen and, to an extent, by Lewis Carroll. Here too, one can observe uncanny similarity between Baum's works and Ray's. Baum was Ray's senior by 31 years, and it is possible that Ray read his writing while a child himself and recognized a kindred spirit.

In *The Wonderful Wizard of Oz*, the Hammer-Heads are a rather small race of unusual and bizarre creatures with very hard, oversized heads, who live on top of a small and rocky hill in the magical Land of Oz. The Hammer-Heads are not very sociable and do not interact with anyone else in Oz, preferring to stick closely to their own kind.

They are extremely independent, quite unfriendly and sometimes even hostile and violent. They do not and will not negotiate, compromise or agree with anyone. They are difficult and disagreeable to outsiders and foreigners. They will not allow any trespassers to cross or pass the rocky hill they live on because it is strictly their rightful turf and territory.

What we have here in Ray's poem, if we assume the number *three* of the three delighted brothers to be significant, is a triumvirate, who are 'brothers', perhaps because they are united by a common cause, and who might possibly share some common characteristics (described in the paragraph above) with the Hammer-Heads – characteristics that assertive nationalism certainly embodied.

Given the timing of the poem, there is a possibility that the triumvirate represents the three leaders of assertive nationalism in India: a trio commonly known as Lal-Bal-Pal (Lala Lajpat Rai, Bal Gangadhar Tilak and Bipin Chandra Pal). They rejected the former methods of the moderate nationalists, i.e., prayers, petitions and pleas to the British government. Instead, they began adopting aggressive measures like *Swadeshi* (indigenous production of goods) and

Boycott (boycott of British-made goods) as means of gaining freedom from British rule in India.

Assertive nationalism, which started around 1908 as a successor movement to the Moderates, persisted up until 1918-19, when it started to fail due to multiple reasons, including arrests of some of its leaders and the retirement from politics of some others.

"Toothless glee" in the poem may very well have been an oblique and inverted reference to assertive nationalism, which in reality was anything but toothless. If universal laughter may have been substituted as symbolic of assertive nationalistic preaching, then we can also find some possible parallels in the assertions in the poem that the trio laugh at everything: one of the stated objectives of assertive nationalism being to infuse the spirit of nationalism among the masses, without regard to occupational, educational or social station.

We have observed in Ray's poetry some very strong nationalistic overtones. Given the timeline of Ray's own prime of youth, he is more likely to have been an assertive nationalist than a moderate, at heart. There are indications in some other poems (e.g., *Babu – The Snake-Charmer*) that Ray may not have been much in favor of passive methods of nationalism.

It is possible that at about the time of composition of this poem, Ray had already begun to see the non-violent influence of Mahatma Gandhi – which he may have considered 'moderate' and ineffective. In the backdrop of the Rowlatt Act, it is not inconceivable that Ray may have wanted to hark back to the contributions of the assertive nationalists.

For readers who might be wondering, the *Jallianwala Bagh* Massacre, also known as the Amritsar Massacre, took place on April 13th, 1919, *after* this poem was published and, therefore, could not have been a trigger for the composition of this poem.

The *Ramgorur* Kid
[Original Bengali: *Ramgorurer Chhana*]

Not much is known about this poem beyond the suggestion that it was meant to poke innocent fun at the solemn and serious practitioners of Brahmoism, an influential religious movement started in Calcutta (now Kolkata) in 1828 by Raja Ram Mohan Roy. The Brahmo Samaj – *samaj*, in Bengali, means community – was led by serious individuals with a reputation for solemnity in demeanor and appearance. In fact, the entire religion had the reputation of shunning the frivolous to a degree.

According to Andrew Robinson, this poem "must surely have been inspired, at least partly, by the solemnity of many Brahmos who surrounded Sukumar in the Samaj."[33] Sukumar Ray had been born into a Brahmo family. We know, however, from the introductory paragraphs to Book Two of this volume, that Ray had a propensity for speaking out against what he considered unnecessary restraints or affected mannerisms. Robinson's comment, while it is an opinion, may likely be true.

It is unknown if Ray chose the name *Ramgorurer Chhana* (literally, the kid – or kids – of a fictitious entity, Ram-Gorur*) to mean the followers of Raja Ram Mohan Roy, or if he meant someone contemporary connected with the Brahmo Samaj. The poem was first published in April-May 1918.

---

*The Bengali *Gorur* is *Garuda*, the mythological bird in Hindu mythology. The prefix *Ram* is meant to signify large or grand. The prefix is comparable to that for an entity like *The Grand Panjandrum*, invented in nonsense verse by British dramatist and actor Samuel Foote around 1755.

Ghostly Play

[Original Bengali: *Bhooturey Khela*]

This poem is very probably satire about Indian art of the Bengal-school, and specifically mocks a watercolor titled *Ganesh Janani* by eminent Bengali artist and writer Abanindranath Tagore.

Towards 1909, a controversy erupted in Bengal over 'unnaturalism' in Indian art, compared to western works. This unnaturalism was the result of prescribed stylistic norms for anatomical depiction, and manifested itself through exaggerated or unrealistically elongated eyes and fingers, exaggerated hips and unnaturally long arms, etc. Debate on the subject continued for the better part of the decade of 1911 and only began to die down towards the beginning of the 1920s.

An example of popular contemporaneous reaction to some of this 'unnaturalism' can be found in a review published in the Bengali periodical, *Sahitya*, at that time, about a watercolor titled *Buddha and Sujata* by famous Bengali artist Abanindranath Tagore. Partha Mitter, in his book *Art and Nationalism in Colonial India 1850-1922 Occidental Orientations* (Cambridge University Press, 1994), writes in his commentary of that review: "The passage [in the review] amused the readers, for they recognized Sujata's unnaturally long arms as referring to the arms of hideous female vampires of Bengali folktales."[34]

Readers of this book familiar with Bengali might be able to work out that the review, in its Bengali original, had been referring to *petni* – the Bengali word for a female ghost. It is obvious from that review in *Sahitya* that a certain portion of the intelligentsia ridiculed the unnatural – sometimes ghost-like – forms created by diktats about human anatomical proportion and artistic metaphors enshrined in conventional Bengal-school styles.

Sukumar Ray was actively involved in speaking out on this controversial subject. He showed a distinct preference for anatomical correctness. Once, in a scathing and sarcastic response to art-critic O. C. Gangoly's support of the conventional Bengal-school ideas, and referring to himself as an "unsubtle man" who failed to understand Gangoly's refined arguments, Ray wrote: "Naturalism, I understand, has no place in Indian art ... [the artist] preferring to ignore the shapes and colours [*sic*] of real objects. He meditates on the theme and paints what appears to the inner eye ... paradoxically, what he sees with the physical eye is a delusion." [35]

'Inner eye' was a concept pioneered by artist Abanindranath Tagore, who was a great proponent of the concept of *bhava* or the *idea* in art. Ray, on the other hand, maintained that to render artistic metaphors (a western example of artistic metaphor would be *hour-glass* waist for a lady) literally, was to reduce them to absurdity.[36]

Abanindranath claimed that his figures obeyed his inner eye. In 1917, he had illustrated this point with a sketch titled *Ankhi Pakhi Dhaay* (The Eye Chases the Bird), in which no bird was to be found, but a young girl was sketched looking out of a window, supposedly looking at a bird. This led to a mocking cartoon by contemporary cartoonist Jatin Sen, titled *The Queen Contemplating the Bird*, which depicted a queen with a caged bird in one hand, but looking in a different direction; the mockery intended being that she was still contemplating the bird, but with her inner-eye.[37] Ray's poem *Ghostly Play*, first published in April-May 1918, within months of this incident, was probably inspired by it.

It is very probable that Ray selected a different – subtly more appropriate – watercolor by Abanindranath, one titled *Ganesh Janani* (Ganesh's Mother; see next page), as the object of his satire.

The theme of this work: mother Parvati holding up the baby elephant-headed godling Ganesh, is strikingly similar to the poem's ghost-mom and her ghostling. This work embodied several of the controversial issues about unnaturalism. In fact, *Sahitya* magazine had also written in ridicule of this painting: "... We are not worried about the elephant-godling but about those painters who hold their brushes in their own elephant-trunks ..."[38]

Ray's redirection of Parvati and Ganesh of the watercolor to ghost-mom and ghostling in the poem was probably inspired by the earlier, female-ghost-invoking, review in *Sahitya* of *Buddha and Sujata*.

The watercolor *Ganesh Janani* depicts Ganesh at play, and a tiny crescent moon at top right, so the phrase "at play by moonlight" in the poem also could be a cryptic reference to this painting.

Ganesh Janani by Abanindranath Tagore.

Throughout the poem, within the endearments that the ghost-mom calls out to her ghostling, are multiple instances of various adjectives that mean plump, e.g., gulpy-cuddle, porky-pudge, doughboy and wild-boar. Plump is not an adjective one culturally associates with ghosts in India; quite the opposite. The elephant-god Ganesh, on the other hand, is well-known for his obesity.

It may be worth mentioning in passing that Ray had also used a direct reference to Ganesh – *gobor-gonesh* – in the original Bengali verse. However, that is an idiomatic usage meaning pudgy, rather than a literal reference to Ganesh, and is therefore, inconclusive.

In his poem, Ray leaves several clues about the presence of satire. First, his reference to "without glasses, saw clear in plain sight" is possibly a mocking reference to Abanindranath's favorite 'inner-eye'. Being an "unsubtle man" Ray sees through the "plain sight" of the physical eye, "without [the] glasses" of the inner-eye.

In the last line of the poem Ray says, "All of a sudden, trick spectral, vanished in a trip-trice!" Earlier, in mocking the 'inner-eye', Ray had said that he saw this vision without glasses and in plain sight. Drawing upon his previous criticism of O. C. Gangoly's views (recall "what [one] sees with the physical eye is a delusion"), Ray's thesis here is that since he saw this vision with physical eyes, it must have been a delusion – a "trick spectral" that vanishes in an instant.

As with other analyses in this volume, this translator does not claim the above to be the correct interpretation. It is meant to suggest a possible line of inquiry as to the poem's hidden meaning, if any.

On a side note, and perhaps a surprising one in the backdrop of their differences of opinion, Ray also translated Abanindranath's Bengali monograph *Murti,* about Bengal-school artistic styles, from Bengali to English, titling it *Indian Iconography*.

Note: In other interpretations of this poem, it has been suggested that the ghostly pair represents emaciated common people after the Bengal famine.[39] However, the periods of the occurrences of the two major famines in Bengal are nowhere near the date of first publication of this poem. Neither, in this translator's opinion, does it seem probable that they would have been subjects of frivolity to be interpreted as satire.

Palm-Mystery
[Original Bengali: *Haat Gonona*]

This poem, most likely, is pure commentary on social evils and superstition. This translator has not been able to decipher another parallel meaning if one was intended.

Here, Uncle Nanda, who earlier, "of worry showed no trace," all of a sudden becomes a "chattering-teeth alarmist" after having visited a palmist and astrologer and been told that he has been living a precarious existence under a harmful combination of astral bodies, and that, therefore, his "life-line [was] full of alarm."

This turns Uncle Nanda from being the smiling, affable man without "any ails or troubles" into one who is "[shivering] frequently [with his] eyes streaming silent tears …," a shadow of his former self.

While it is quite inappropriate to laugh at Uncle Nanda's plight, Ray probably meant this poem for his young readers, to humorously drive home the point that superstition was illogical, and to be avoided.

No concealed commentary could be unearthed. The poem was first published in June-July 1918.

Sense of Essence
[Original Bengali: *Gondho Bichar*]

It is likely that this poem is a parody of a scandal in English parliament in 1922 regarding the sale of honors by the then prime minister David Lloyd George and members of his cabinet.

No direct clues are available to indicate if this poem has any hidden meaning. The narrative of the poem is simple enough, and it is obviously funny. One has very sparse clues that are rather indirect in the narrative.

Since the poem is about a questionable 'stench' in court, emanating from a dignitary no less than the prime minister, one might suppose it may have had to do with some scandal in government in the highest quarters. The fact that it starts with "Mounted the king his royal throne," may point towards a scandal in the court of a newly crowned monarch, involving some high official in government.

That everyone who is being asked to investigate the stench is finding an excuse to avoid doing so, might be a veiled indicator that those being tasked with discovery may have somehow been complicit in the cause.

Trying to resort to our trusty method of looking for potential satire-worthy events preceding the first publication date of the poem, we run into a problem: this poem was *not* previously published in *Sandesh* magazine, and while a first publication date may be available somewhere, this translator has not been able to find it.

However, a likely guess is near 1922-1923, since the poem had not been seen in earlier years, and Abol Tabol was compiled in 1923.

There is another possible avenue of inquiry as to the date of the event if we take "Mounted the king his royal throne, chimed bells the ascension" literally, and look for a British monarch having ascended the throne. This is not much help, since George V was crowned emperor in 1910, and reigned till 1936. So, no ascensions during the time that this poem may have been composed.

Nevertheless, there is one scandal in British parliament in 1922, that might qualify. This was the scandal over the practice of sale, for money, of honors, i.e., knighthoods, baronetcies and peerages.

Prime Minister Lloyd George's government had been engaging in this practice for some time, without much quality control of the recipients, other than their ability to pay. Noting that there were men with cash to spare who couldn't quite afford a knighthood, Lloyd George's government specifically invented the Order of the British Empire (OBE) to fill the gap in the market. As a result, 25,000 people were 'awarded' the OBE over a period of four years, and the 'honor' became so rapidly devalued that it was commonly derisively known as the Order of the Bad Egg.[40] The suggestion of a disagreeable smell (from bad eggs regarding the sale of honors) is our first inkling of the stench that this poem may be referring to.

Had the PM been questioned about this by the king, though? Apparently so. The tipping-point in Lloyd George's scheme was reached with the announcement of the July 1922 honors list. This included the award of honors to John Drughorn (convicted in 1915 for trading with the enemy), William Vestey (convicted of tax evasion) and a peerage for Joseph Robinson (a South African who had only recently been fined £500,000 for his role in a share fraud) for "imperial and public services." This was too much for King George V, who complained that "the Robinson case must be regarded as little less than an insult to Crown and to the House of Lords."[41] Robinson was forced to refuse the peerage, with the utmost reluctance. George V demanded an explanation from his PM.

Apparently, Lloyd George initially attempted to plead that the sale of honors was a traditionally common occurrence and nothing out of the ordinary (he wasn't entirely incorrect).[42] King James II had started it all by putting a price tag on baronetcies in the 17th century, and the practice did not quite die out in later years either*. The PM's response in the poem, "Daubed essence, your Maj." (implying a common practice), combined with the latter part of the original Bengali line which literally translated would have read: 'the smell's not so bad', might refer to this defense.

This theory does fall short of accounting for the "King's brother-in-law." There is no indication that any of the three brothers of Queen Mary could have been involved in this scandal. It is possible, however, that Ray did not mean the king's brother in law in the literal sense at all, but simply meant to imply some of the characters above, who had been detained at His Majesty's pleasure – 'king's son-in-law' being a rare, close Bengali idiomatic usage meaning the same.

After Lloyd George's coalition government was decisively voted out by the Conservatives in October 1922, he was succeeded by Andrew Bonar Law as Prime Minister. Immediately prior to this, Bonar Law had held the position of Chancellor of the Exchequer – so, indeed, "King's [old[†], i.e., previous] treasurer."

---

* "More recently, Harold Wilson also dished out peerages to those who were prepared to dig deeply into their pockets. Indeed, his resignation honours [*sic*] list was so controversial that one contemporary wrote "he brought so much discredit to the system that it might not survive in its present form." ... In the Thatcher years, peerages were given to 11 private sector industrialists whose companies gave total donations of £1.9m to Conservative funds. In addition 44 other industrialists whose companies gave a total of £4.4m to Tory funds received knighthoods." – *Wales Online,* U.K. Dec. 2006, updated Mar. 2013.

† Bonar Law wasn't exactly very old – he was 64 in 1922 – but had earlier, in 1921, resigned from his post due to ill-health. He was Britain's shortest-serving prime-minister, having resigned again in mid-1923, after serving exactly seven months. He died the same year, from cancer of the throat.

Trivia: Ray was certainly not the last to milk the scandal for humor: In *The Inimitable Jeeves* (1924) by famous English author P G Wodehouse, the character Bingo Little bemoaned that peerages were "costing the deuce – even baronetcies have gone up frightfully nowadays, I am told."

The Tomcat's Song
[Original Bengali: *Hulor Gaan*]

This poem, first published in July-August 1919, is absolutely crying out loud that it is satire. It has been extremely frustrating to note the presence of what might be clues but be unable to relate them to an event that may have been the subject of that satire. Like for several other poems in this volume, the exercise of sleuthing it out will have to be left to the enthusiastic reader.

The reasons why this translator suspects satire are the following:

Firstly, we have a narrative that very much might be allegory. The tomcat has hidden a piece of pancake to be eaten later, but when he goes to retrieve it, he finds that his stash has already been raided by another cat. This could easily have been a parody of contemporaneous events.

Secondly, the fact that the tomcat has a sort of understudy friend, may be indicative of the existence of a follower, duo or group who may have been thus swindled by a rival group or individual.

Thirdly, there are indications that the tomcat had forgotten about the pancake, i.e., neglected something important, while being engaged in other pursuits – symbolized by singing songs. Upon loss of opportunity – which enraged some other, close, interested party ("missus, thunderous") –, the poor tomcat has to, sadly, go back to singing "cat-song doleful."

Some other clues worth noting while looking for contemporaneous events that may have been mocked or parodied, are the following:

One, it seems from her name that the thieving cat was female, while our protagonist is certainly male (the Bengali word *hulo*, used to identify our protagonist in the Bengali original, specifically denotes tomcat). Male and female may be real, or metaphors for the attitudes of the characters. (Sexism wasn't yet a 'thing' back then).

Two, the name for the thief in the original Bengali is *'Neki'*. *Neki* is the female form of the Bengali word *nyaka*, which has no direct translation in English, but means a person who displays a simpering, affectedly innocent mannerism and an intentional but false, i.e., bogus, cluelessness. Whether this may be significant in identifying the rival person or group, we do not know; but it could very well be.

Three, *Neki* is described to be 'clip-eared'; literally, *kan-kata* in the Bengali original. *Kan-kata*, however, also *idiomatically* means 'shameless', in Bengali. Perhaps that information might aid in identification, as well. Note, significantly, that Ray's original manuscript did *not* have this reference to *kan-kata*; he added it later, prior to the poem's publication in *Sandesh* magazine.[43]

As to whether the environmental setting: "mystic, bare night quietness lapped" is in itself a clue, this translator is, well, clueless.

Cry-Kid

[Original Bengali: *Knaduney*]

This translator has not been able to figure this poem out.

The narrative would tend to indicate that Ray's purpose – if there was an ulterior one – was to mock some phenomenally loud complainer. That this complainer is of British origin is also almost certain, since he is the child of Mr. and Mrs. Booth. That he resides in India – may be somewhere in Bengal – is also likely, since the Booths are neighbors of the Bengali gentleman, Nondo Ghosh.

It is worth mentioning that the illustration accompanying this poem is somewhat intriguing. First of all, observing the style of drawing, it does tend to call in question whether it had originally been drawn by Ray at all. Its style is more reminiscent of contemporary cartoons that appeared in the British magazine *Punch*, rather than typical of illustrations by Ray. We know from our analysis of the poem *The Delighted,* that Ray has been known to borrow – albeit rarely – illustrations by others when the situation warranted it. In the case of that illustration, the drawing was unsigned – something not typical of Ray's other illustrations. Our current poem, *Cry-Kid*, was first published in *Sandesh* magazine in the April-May 1919 issue. The illustration accompanying this poem in that issue of *Sandesh* is also unsigned. Also intriguing is the fact that the illustration in *Sandesh* is different from the one that appears in the later compilation, Abol Tabol. The original *Sandesh* magazine illustration depicts a bawling child being stood up on his mother's knees in the foreground, with what is presumably the child's father holding a newspaper and sitting in an armchair, in the background. The illustration in the Abol Tabol compilation – also unsigned* - does away with the father in the armchair and retains only the mother and child.

---

* Surprisingly, in a subsequent edition of Abol Tabol published by *Bidyamandir* (Calcutta, 1930), Ray's signature magically reappears on this illustration. Unverified conjecture is that it may have been added by an overzealous art-editor unaware that Ray had left in unsigned.

Left: Original illustration in *Sandesh* magazine.
Right: The final illustration in Abol Tabol.

Therefore, given the fact that Ray had, in 1923, curated the poems of the Abol Tabol compilation from previously published poems, and had also edited several of them in the process (for relevance to their intended messaging in Abol Tabol) it would tend to indicate that only the mother-and-child portion of the drawing is relevant to his intended message.

Interestingly, comparing the original (in *Sandesh*) and the subsequent illustration, it is easy to see that they are, in fact, two different drawings. The illustration in *Sandesh* differs subtly from the later illustration in the shape of the child's arms, the size of his face, the shape of the mother's face and body, the placement of the mother's chair, the angle of the rug and so on. In the case of the poem *The Delighted*, Ray had redrawn Denslow's art. It appears that he may have done the same for the art accompanying *Cry-Kid*, possibly at the time of compiling Abol Tabol.

Also worth noting is the fact that the last two lines of the poem published in *Sandesh* are different from the last two lines in the version edited by Ray for Abol Tabol. In the version in *Sandesh,* the last two lines, roughly translated, read as follows:

"Wah-hooh; hoo waa-waah, hoo-hooah-wah-hah-hose,
Will wallow in ink, chew reading glasses; bite dad on the nose!"

The same two lines in the Abol Tabol version read:

"Fearsome noise, that haunted places of ghosts can rid,
Impressed to the core I am; what a phenomenal cry-kid!"

In several other poems, such as *Knotty Woodoo, Battle Crazed* and *The Tomcat's Song*, Ray had made edits to the originals in order to make the poems of Abol Tabol better reflect his messaging. The sarcasm evident in the last line of the Abol Tabol version in this case is clue enough that satire was intended towards some targeted entity.

The entity targeted is obviously represented by the crying kid being stood up on the knees of a European lady, presumably Mrs. Booth. Had this been during the reign of a female monarch in England, one could have pursued historical lines of inquiry based on the assumption that the complainer was a political entity who complained loudly to the Queen, but that is a dead-end since the reigning monarch at that time was male – George V. That is not to say we should ignore the illustration altogether, but perhaps need an alternate line of inquiry.

Also, it is *not* imperative that the son of the Booths be English. It is possible that Ray may have mocked some anglophile Indian personage as 'son of the Booths'. Admittedly, the probability of that is low, though, since: (1) in other poems, Ray has used the maternal uncle-nephew relationship to symbolize British-Indian relationships; not that of mother-son, and (2) from her dress in the illustration accompanying the poem, it appears that the mother of the crying child is a western lady (granted, however, that an Indian 'child' complaining to 'mother' British empire is not entirely impossible).

Something else to keep in mind, however: 'Nondo Ghosh' may have been used by Ray as another way to refer to himself, or more accurately, to the narrator of the poem. This is not particularly intuitive, but it does work in the Bengali language. It is possible to derive from the Bengali saying, *'Joto dosh, Nondo Ghosh!'*, meaning, 'For every ill, I get blamed!'. In the accepted meaning of that saying, *Nondo Ghosh* – a proper noun – is the name of a person who is a fictious-entity representation of the pronoun "I".

If Ray had intended *Nondo Ghosh* to mean "I" and not a particular person of that name, that complicates matters somewhat: Is this "I" just one person, and Mr. Booth is his or her neighbor somewhere in Bengal, or does "I" represent all of India, and Mr. Booth is a sort of 'neighbor' by virtue of being under the same government, and may represent someone in England, or the common people of England?

Those are some of the other considerations one would need to keep in mind while pursuing inquiry into the possible presence of a hidden message in the poem.

Overall, given the length of the poem and its narrative, this translator strongly suspects satire. He just has not been able to figure it out.

Fear Not

[Original Bengali: *Bhoy Peona*]

Fear Not is a poem that easily gives away the fact that it is political satire. Of course, if one was not looking for an inner meaning, one could be forgiven for assuming that it is just another hilariously funny poem.

Given Ray's propensity for mocking the British in his poems at every opportunity, it can be clearly surmised in the context that the horned beast with the cudgel is a thinly veiled metaphor for the ruling British in India trying to reassure Indians that they have the Indians' best interests at heart.

Fear Not was first published in June-July 1918. True to the pattern of Ray's political satire lagging historical events by six to twelve months, one can find that in August 1917, in recognition of India's support during World War I and in response to renewed nationalist demands, Edwin Montagu, the then British Secretary of State for India, had made the historic announcement in Parliament that, going forward, the British policy for India would be to have "increasing association of Indians in every branch of the administration and the gradual development of self-governing institutions with a view to the progressive realisation [*sic*] of responsible government in India as an integral part of the British Empire."

It is entirely possible that Ray intended to mock this announcement, and even suggest that no good would come of it for the Indians. The supposedly hesitant invitee into the beast's "burrow" (*lair* was probably implied) is obviously meant to represent the wary Indian populace, and embodies Ray's skepticism of this British overture. The British still held all the power (the cudgel or club in the poem). Ray also probably suggests that even this increasing association of Indians in administration would be accomplished through forcible cooperation or, essentially, coercion, and that Indians risked retribution if they did not cooperate. Note the imperious: "Together we'll bite you. Be unafraid – at once!"

Since Ray drew his own illustrations, it is easy to see that Ray depicted the British (or perhaps, Montagu) as the devil, with three horns, probably mirroring Lucifer's trident.*

The reference to "me, the missus and my brood of nine sons" does not present any obvious clues and may be open to interpretation. Without drawing any definite conclusions, below are some facts:

In 1915, Montagu married Venetia Stanley, daughter of Edward Stanley, 4th Baron Stanley of Alderley. Stanley's marriage to Montagu was an unhappy one, and she was reported to have had multiple affairs, both pre and post-marriage.

Bobbie Neate, in her book *Conspiracy of Secrets* (John Blake, 2012), suggests that Montagu's and Stanley's marriage was a lavender marriage of social convenience, as a cover, both for Montagu's homosexuality and Stanley's earlier affair with Asquith who served as Prime Minister of the United Kingdom from 1908 to 1916.[44]

It is not clear how much of the above information was generally known at that time. British press in those days was usually reticent about printing gossip involving a PM. However, Ray had lived in England during the period 1911 to 1913 and may have known about some of it. Ray was a friend of the Indian mathematician Prasanta Mahalanobis, who was at the Kings College, University of Cambridge, when Ray was in England. Another individual who was also at the same institution at that time was the closet homosexual economist John Maynard Keynes. Keynes had been a close friend of Edwin Montagu since 1909.

If Ray was, indeed, aware of Montagu's homosexuality, then his reference to "nine sons" could have been meant as an unkind joke on

---

* Lucifer does, indeed, have a trident, although in popular illustrations the devil is often portrayed with a two-pronged pitchfork rather than a trident.

the extreme remoteness of the possibility that the Edwin-Venetia couple would produce a child at all.*

This translator is not entirely certain if the stanza "Fear you these horns that out of my head jut? / I suffer from brain ailment, I don't head-butt" had anything to do with the alleged aspect of Montagu's sexual orientation.

The "nine sons" could also have referred to Montagu's 15-member Council of India, of which at least nine members were required, by mandate, to have appropriate "Indian Qualifications."[45] However, this is unlikely as it would not explain the "missus."

---

* In reality, a child, Judith, was born, in 1923. Legally and socially, Judith was Montagu's daughter, but she is rumored to have been fathered by William Humble Eric Ward, then Viscount Ednam, and later, 3rd Earl of Dudley.

Crass Cow
[Original Bengali: *Tnyash Goru*]

The original Bengali title of *Crass Cow* is *Tnyash Goru*. The word *goru*, in Bengali, means cow. *Tnyash* is a derogatory word that means hybrid or mixture, but is usually used to denote 'westernized', in an unkind sort of way.

The first clue that this poem is social satire is embedded in its title itself. This is a poem meant to lampoon those Indians who were over-eager to appear sophisticated and conformist by being westernized or aping their British colonizers. This theme appears time and again in Ray's poetry, in poems like *Mutant Medley*, *Wacky No-One* and *Hookah-Face Hyangla*.

The confirmation of Ray's intent comes in the very first line, which says that this animal is not "bovine, but a bird," in reality. Indians aping the British are compared to birds trying to be cows. However, Ray has many more messages about such individuals, woven skillfully into the description of Crass Cow and her characteristics.

The heavy-lidded eyes point to her having shut out reality. It also conveys the impression of Crass Cow looking down upon others, with a supercilious air, through half-closed eyes. The black hair "combed in style" probably refers to the westernized Indian habit of applying pomade to hair. Pomades like the French product Brilliantine, created at the turn of the 20th century, were popular among a section of English gentlemen of that time. Ray's self-drawn illustration accompanying the poem shows Crass Cow with a headful of hair with middle-parting – another popular style with the English in the 1920s.

Poushali Bhadury in her essay *Fantastic Beasts and How to Sketch Them: The Fabulous Bestiary of Sukumar Ray*, provides a remarkably perspicacious analysis of this poem; reproduced below:

"The first information readers are given is that the tynash [*sic*] goru, with the head of a cow and the wings and feet of a bird, is in fact a bird. The implication, of course, is that even the creature itself does not know what it is and recognizes only a tiny part of its hybrid identity. Moreover, it is extremely significant that Ray's tynash goru is for sale to the highest bidder; the verses are presented as a sales advertisement, detailing its various charms. Readers see here a negative, satiric portrait of a hybrid personage as a sell-out that refuses to recognize the very unique subject-position it occupies. ... ... The specific choice of a cow, generally regarded as a domesticated, passive beast that does not show any initiative or intelligence of its own and is raised only to serve humans, is a significant one. It allows Ray to pictorially portray to an even greater degree the tynash goru's unthinking meekness, which within a British colonial context, becomes a dangerous form of compliance to an oppressive and unjust foreign authority.

In fact, the verse references to the tynash goru's delicate digestive system, its shaky legs, slack joints, wheezy breaths or its tendency periodically to burst out sobbing for no discernible reason, complement the illustration in underscoring the lack of strength, courage and independent thinking that characterizes this biddable beast. The illustration depicts the creature as so significantly top-heavy and lopsided that readers are left wondering how the tynash goru even manages to stand up in a balanced fashion, let alone move around properly. The spindly bird-legs and cow's tail of the back torso, in such ungainly contrast to the significantly more imposing head, neck and front wings of the beast, visually represent the uneasy balance of various different attributes—comprising both Bengali manners and those "borrowed" from British customs—that the tynash goru emblematizes. The ponderous quality of this hybrid creature, depicted in the verses, is also conveyed visually [*in Ray's illustration – clarification translator's*] by excessive use of shading and cross-hatching to present a "heavier" picture that is mostly in shadow.

The scarf around its neck (present in the illustration, though not mentioned in the verses) completes the picture of absurdity and adds to Ray's pointed satire: it seems that aside from the attributes of a cow and a bird, this creature wishes to mimic some human fashions too."

– Bhadury, P. *Fantastic Beasts and How to Sketch Them:*
The Fabulous Bestiary of Sukumar Ray
(South Asian Review, Vol. 34, No. 1, 2013, 24-25).
Reproduced above under fair use guidelines of copyrighted material.

Contemporaneous Bengali literature contains many instances of characters such as those represented by Crass Cow going to extreme lengths to deride and avoid traditional Indian customs, mannerisms, dress and food habits. This translator believes that the scarf around Crass Cow's neck may have been meant to signify the Crass Cow's attempt to protect herself from 'catching a cold' of anything Indian or native. If so, the line "Touch her, and she moos out loud in shocked dread" also makes perfect sense.

There appears to be room for speculation about the stanza, "Only candles and soap-soup eats the contrarian." Mulligatawny soup (from the Indian Tamil-language *mulug* (lentils) and *thanni* (water)) was popular among the British in India during Ray's time. Some varieties of lentils, e.g. pigeon-peas (*arhar daal* or *toor daal* as called in India) tend to impart a soapy texture to soup prepared with them. While, admittedly, pigeon-peas were not the default variety of lentil for preparing mulligatawny soup, their possible used cannot be ruled out. On another extended flight of fancy, one might focus also on the coriander (more popularly known in the USA as cilantro) leaves that were often used as garnish atop mulligatawny soup. To a significant portion of the human population – those who carry the gene named OR6A2 in their DNA – coriander leaves are known to taste like soap.

Had Sukumar Ray previously tasted mulligatawny soup garnished with coriander and referred to it as "soap-soup"? Dare one speculate, therefore, on whether he carried the offending gene in his DNA? This translator prefers to steer clear of creating yet another controversy!

What 'candles' referred to in the stanza initially appeared unclear. One could consider the possibility of them being symbolic of sausages, perhaps. However, on second thoughts, they probably refer to soup-sticks* (better known as breadsticks in the USA), which have had a history of being popularly served along with soup, since as early as the mid-seventeenth century.

The intended meanings of "Horns shaped like 'threes'; tail, a spiral thread" are difficult to decipher, but there are some clues and possible explanations:

In the matter of the shape of horns, Ray was referring to the Bengali numeral three. This is written in Bengali somewhat like the trademark Nike 'swoosh', but mirrored laterally, i.e., reversed left to right, like this: '৩'. Multiple minor variations – such as flatter, laterally elongated versions – are common. Ray's illustration accompanying this poem depicts Crass Cow with such horns.

If one were to attribute the use of the word 'horns' to denote a derisive reference to hats worn by the English, then, comparing the broadside silhouette views of the fashionably twisted *brims* of popular hat styles of those times (see image, next page) – tops hats, bowlers, homburgs – one can, with very little stretch of imagination, discern the shape of the Bengali numeral three, in different variations. It is possible, even if perhaps far-fetched, that Crass Cow's horns, "shaped like [Bengali] threes" referred to such hats worn in imitation of English gentlemen.

The reference to "tail a spiral thread" could, admittedly with a major leap of imagination, have referred to tailcoats popular in those times (especially the split-tail ones). However, this translator has no explanation to suggest as to why those tails might have been spiral.

Men's hat styles, 1920s, showing
brims that look like the Bengali numeral three ['৩'].

Walking-sticks with decoratively twisted shafts, especially when combined with certain postures adopted by their owners while stationary and leaning on them, might qualify better, provided, of course, there was a preponderance of that design rather than the straight-shafted variety in those times. The poem was first published in February-March 1922.

---

* This translator is indebted to Kankona Mukherjee and Shovan Choudhuri of the Facebook Group titled *Sukumar Ray Club* for having first pointed out the possibility of "candles" representing soup-sticks, which assistance he acknowledges with thanks.

Notebook
[Original Bengali: *Noteboi*]

This poem appears to be one more example of Ray poking fun at know-it-alls and wannabe know-it-alls. This contempt is seen oft repeated in several poems in Abol Tabol. The poems *Caution* and *Explanations* immediately come to mind.

In this poem, we have a wannabe know-it-all attempting to appear important with his claim that he has a notebook in which he "write[s] down instant[ly] as [he hears] new facts." He then gives examples of several such 'facts' which are patently too comically ludicrous for anyone to chronicle.

He then goes on to ask some equally ludicrous questions for which no one would normally know the answers and asserts that the reason for people not knowing the answers is that they have not read his (obviously very important) notebook.

The purpose, once again, is to make Ray's younger readers aware of the existence of such people and enable the readers to recognize them. By making such people appear ridiculous, Ray conditions his young readers to view such personalities with skepticism.

It is not known if this poem might be satire on some official entity spying upon the populace and noting down details of everything, which notes might later be analyzed by his superiors to determine if any of it indicated seditious behavior.

Alternatively, it has also been conjectured* – but not known with any degree of certainty – that the owner of the notebook, who extensively catalogues "facts" or statistics, is humorously modelled after Ray's mathematician and statistician friend Prasanta Mahalanobis.

---

* First suggested to this translator by Debasis Mukhopadhyay of Chandannagar, West Bengal, India, which suggestion he acknowledges with thanks.

(M)address
[Original Bengali: *Tthikana*]

Delightfully funny, this poem is about a person asking for the address of another, whom he goes into major roundabout relationship-references to identify.

The response is equally funny, when his respondent takes him through a rigmarole of directions, only to bring him back to his starting point, and then delivers his reason for doing what he did: "don't bother me."

This translator is unable to discern if there is any other meaning intended in the poem than the overt one. A first-publication date for this poem is not available, which makes the identification of any potential event that may have been mocked all the more difficult.

However, possibly in the same vein as several other poems, it too, perhaps, contains commentary on (a) ineffectual Indian politicians negotiating everything *other than* what they really wanted: e.g. negotiating for *Swaraj* (self-governance) and Home Rule rather than independence (in the first part of the poem) and (b) equivocation on the part of the British government, leading negotiations back to square one (in the second part of the poem).

It has also been suggested that the poem points to rootlessness and a sense of alienation and loss of identity among Indian people during British times.[46] However, this translator has not been able to commit to the leap of imagination required to accept that explanation.

Strongman
[Original Bengali: *Palowan*]

This poem was probably written in tribute of the legendary Bengali wrestler and strongman, Bhim Bhabani, shortly after his untimely death.

During the 1920s, there prevailed significant interest in the sport of wrestling in Bengal. One of the all-time greats from Bengal was strongman Bhim Bhabani (born Bhabendramohan Saha in 1890).

Bhim Bhabani got his start at the gymnasium (Bengali translation: *aakhdaa*) run by the well-known trainer Khetu Babu, at the locality of Darjipara in Calcutta (now Kolkata), in Bengal. In later life, Bhim Bhabani trained in bodybuilding under Professor* Kodi Ramamurthy Naidu and then joined the Hippodrome Circus owned by Professor† Krishnalal Basak.

Bhim Bhabani made a name for himself in the circus, and is credited with being the first strongman to demonstrate supporting an elephant on a cushioned plank of wood on his chest for more than a minute at a time.[47] He was also known for placing 40-*maund* (~1.5tons / 3,300lbs) weight of stones on his chest, and having an ensemble of 20-25 musicians sit atop it and sing renditions from Indian *ragas*. He could also prevent two motorcars from moving, by holding onto them with his hands.[48]

Bhim Bhabani's breakfast comprised one *chhatak* (57gm / 2oz) of *ghee* (clarified butter), 2 *seers* (1.9kg / 4.1lbs) of meat and a sherbet prepared from 200 peanuts.[49] Lunch was a relatively simple affair with an "appropriate" portion of rice and lentils. Fruit worth Rupees 2.00 – 2.50 in those days (approximately USD 8.00 – USD 10.00 in

*† A self-adopted honorific; its use a practice common among eminent personalities connected with circus and physical sports in those days.

2020 terms), a *seer* of meat and a sherbet of 50 peanuts constituted high-tea, followed by dinner consisting of *chappatis* (the "flatbread" mentioned in the poem) made from half a *seer* of wheat-flour, along with three-quarters of a *seer* of meat. [50]

Apart from Bhim Bhabani's superhuman strength and diet that find parallels with those of the strongman's in the poem, the fact that the locale Darjipara (where *Khetu Babu's Aakhdaa* – Bhim Bhabani's training ground – was located) and the place Beniatola mentioned in the last line of the poem are geographically adjacent and essentially abut each other, is of no small significance in pointing to a connection between Bhim Bhabani and the poem. Also interestingly, Ray's illustration accompanying the poem depicts the strongman holding a mace which isn't shaped like a mace at all but rather like a 'globe barbell' at which Bhim Bhabani was an acknowledged master. The illustration also depicts the strongman as dressed in tiger-skin. Popular photographs of Bhim Bhabani during his lifetime show him wearing the same. [51]

Bhim Bhabani died in 1922 at the relatively young age of 32. Given that this poem was first published in August-September 1923, it was likely composed six or a few more months earlier; hence, very possibly triggered by Bhim Bhabani's untimely death, and as eulogy and tribute to his achievements.

This translator is indebted to Debajyoti Guha of Kolkata, India for alerting the translator to the possibility of a connection between Bhim Bhabani and this poem, which assistance he acknowledges with thanks.

Learning Science
[Original Bengali: *Bigyan Shikkha*]

First-published in September-October 1919, this poem is very probably satire triggered by The Sadler Commission Report to the Government, published the same year. The Sadler Commission, headed by Dr. M. E. Sadler, Vice Chancellor of the University of Leeds, had been appointed in 1917 to study and report on the problems of Calcutta University.

Note that despite its narrative about a young boy's head being examined, the title of the poem is not Scientific Examination, but, rather, *Learning Science*. It could also have translated to 'Teaching Science'. Ray invents a clever device he calls the *'futoscope'*, the purpose of which is to provide visibility into the victim's brain. Ray's self-drawn illustration accompanying the poem suggests a hollow tube with no lens, for this *futoscope*. The hollow tube, in place of a real scope, was probably meant to illustrate the satire, if Ray had believed that the Sadler Commission was either unnecessary or incompetent.

Ray's satire on 'hollowness' of the commission is somewhat at odds with the effect that Sir Asutosh Mookerjee, the then Vice-Chancellor of the university, derived out of it, however. British bureaucracy was frequently at odds with Sir Asutosh over university administration and had tried to exclude him from the commission. J. Lourdusamy, in his book *Science and National Consciousness in Bengal 1870-1930* (Orient Longman, 2004), writes, "However, Mookerjee was on good terms with the chairman of the commission, Michael Sadler ... and succeeded in having almost all of his central ideas incorporated into the commission's final recommendations."[52]

On another level, considering the decidedly Indian attire of the 'examiner' and the western clothing worn by the young boy in the illustration, Ray may have been suggesting that Sadler was an academic novice compared to the stature of Sir Asutosh, and, in reality, the former ought to be examined by latter.

Missed!

[Original Bengali: *Foshke Gelo!*]

This poem was first published in May-June 1919. It is possible that it was inspired by the accidental demise of the magician Chung Ling Soo at the Wood Green Empire theater in London in March 1918. While it cannot be claimed with certainty, the character *Gosttho Mama* in the poem is probably none other than Chung Ling Soo.

In historical research, the Wood Green Empire incident, shows up as a notable event of 1918 even today. The opening stanza of the poem, "Oh, come see what's about to be; / watch this show, magical spree / Some trickery; deceit wee ...", also tends to point towards a show or performance involving magic or trickery.

Magician Chung Ling Soo's real name was William Ellsworth Campbell Robinson. He was an American, who had established a decent practice in London as a stage-magician disguised as a Chinese, in the process also having had appropriated part of the name of another real Chinese magician, Ching Ling Foo.[53] One of the main attractions of his repertoire was an act titled *Condemned to Death by the Boxers* (after the Boxer Rebellion), during the performance of which Robinson's assistant would fire a musket at the magician, who would then proceed to either 'swallow' the musket-ball or catch it and drop it in a basket.

In reality, not a musket-ball, but a cartridge comprising a bullet backed with its own built-in charge was used. The musket had been modified too, of course, and was equipped with an additional concealed barrel. The main barrel, containing gunpowder, produced the flash and bang. The actual bullet, while ceremoniously shown as being rammed into the barrel prior to the trick, was secretly inserted into the additional barrel that was not filled with gunpowder and not intended to fire.

On March 23, 1918, due to the use of an improperly cleaned real (firing) barrel, the flash also ignited the built-in charge of the bullet in what was supposed to be the dud (non-firing) adjacent barrel, causing the bullet to fire and hit Robinson in the chest, thereby causing his death.[54]

In Ray's illustrations accompanying the poem, although a bow and arrow are depicted instead of a musket, those could easily be symbolic stand-ins for the musket and bullet. *Gosttho Mama* is wearing decidedly western dress (recall Ray's propensity for dressing westerners in western attire in his illustrations), probably indicating the westerner, Robinson. He wears shorts, however, and not full trousers – probably a passing reference to his having had appropriated a Chinese identity – so, in reality, only half-western. His shoes appear to bear strong resemblance to pictures of old Chinese footwear made of wood. He appears in the illustration complete with a basket (into which Robinson was meant to catch and drop the bullet), and there is no mistaking that his face in the illustration has been drawn with a decidedly Chinese cast.

Moreover, the bow is held by the assistant incorrectly – back to front – possibly symbolic of the error of the improperly cleaned musket.

The attire of the assistant, admittedly, is difficult to fit entirely into this narrative. His clothes, consisting of long trousers and a tunic with slanted buttoned closure are, indeed, very reminiscent of the attire of Boxer rebels portrayed in contemporaneous art, but it is difficult to explain what appears to be a medal or patch on the left side of his chest. The fact that he wears spectacles is probably also significant, but its import difficult to discover. This leads this translator to conjecture that perhaps, in yet another example of his multilayered thinking, Ray had potentially drawn parallels with Robinson's accidental death to some additional contemporaneous incident, clues to which are possibly embedded in the illustration, still waiting to be discovered.

Droplets
[Untitled in the Bengali original]

These seven quatrains were first published in *Sandesh* magazine in the issues of April-May 1921 and May-June 1922, as untitled, page-filler rhymes, under the category *Chhnitephnota*,[55] meaning 'iota' or 'jot', but loosely translatable as 'Droplets'. The Bengali word *chhnitephnota* literally translates to tiny, spattered droplets.

When published in the compilation Abol Tabol, these droplets continued to remain untitled. This translator has chosen to call this collection of seven 'droplets' together, simply, *Droplets*.

Daring to assume any of Ray's poems in Abol Tabol as harmlessly harboring no other than its overt meaning is probably folly. With that in mind, this translator cautions that if there are hidden messages embedded in these quatrains, he has, sadly, not been able to decipher them.

Even based on their literal meanings, which could very well be parodies of somethings else, their potential for being some kind of commentary remains high.

Muse of Whimsy
[Original Bengali: *Abol Tabol*]

Poignant is not a word that normally springs to mind when discussing the contents of Abol Tabol. However, this is the most poignant poem in the collection. Ray wrote this poem about himself – and also about his verse – while on his deathbed. This poem was his last ever composition. Ray died young, of an initially misdiagnosed illness that had few treatment options available in his time. Sadly, this is clearly a poem composed by a man who has already made his peace with the fact that his days in this world are numbered.

However, the poem is also Ray's own cleverly hidden affirmation of the presence of satire embedded in the poems of Abol Tabol. Ray told not just one, but two stories through this poem. The poem, in fact, is a work of genius, with three layers of meaning: the literal, the implied and the covert. The literal is evident in the poem's words. We shall focus, below, on the implied and the covert.

The early stanzas of the poem point to the good times that the poet has had on earth, where "in playful-tuned whimsies, [he] trill[ed] joyful fancies." However, he also indicates that the joyful fancies that he trills are sung at a place where "forbids, no constraint / No barrier, no restraint," that is, in his private world of disguised satire. There he can do what he likes – float his dreamboats under painted skies – meaning, he can speak his mind under the guise of nonsense verse. In it, the unreal or imaginary (a direct idiomatic translation of the Bengali '*akash-kushum*') becomes real. The '*akash-kushum*' (literally, *cosmic blossom*) '*aapni fote*', meaning, blooms by itself, to signify that the hidden messages in his poems reveal themselves. And, when they do, they enlighten and amaze the reader: "Sense and sky tinted – [with delight] / [In] reveal[ed] wonders unstinted."

At the end of this part, Ray makes tacit acknowledgement of the fact that it is time to go, but that he would like, before he "must go", to "Say what's on [his] mind so." It is almost certain that here Ray was also having himself a private laugh. The original lines, literally translated, say the following about what Ray wishes to share: 'It does not matter if they make no sense / Does not matter if *not everyone* can understand them'. It could not be clearer that Ray was referring not only to the whimsy of his nonsense verse, but also to the satire hidden in his poems, which, he knew, that perhaps *not everyone* would understand. Quite a significant departure from his earlier insistence that Abol Tabol 'was conceived in the spirit of whimsy'.

The tone of the language in this poem takes a sudden turn at this point from the dulcet, lilting rhythm that had gone before, to an aggressive, galloping cadence with a quicker tempo, even as the meter remains unchanged. Contrast the tonal qualities of the two adjacent stanzas: the slow, "I cast off, and my boat row / Where whimsies ebb and flow" and the quick, "The sprinting word who can rein? / Who today would me restrain?" This transition takes the reader by surprise. It is ironic, that perhaps without intending to, Ray ended up parodying the shock that the revelation that he had contracted an 'incurable' disease at such a young age must have delivered. Or it may have been in deliberate symbolic defiance of the blow that fate had dealt him. It clearly is also a cryptic reference indicating that the 'sprinting' satire concealed in Ray's verse cannot be 'restrained'.

The stanzas that follow are simple enough, where it is clear that Ray's verse implies his own particular forte: words, deployed in a mastery of sound and rhyme, to expound the myriad ideas that keep bubbling up in his mind: "In the midst today of my mind, / Beats a drum of a lively kind." To be fair, here Ray wrote *tabla*, a different instrument, but juxtapose this with the possible covert meaning that what beats today in his mind is a drum of revolution – the *'maadol'*, from our earlier analysis of the very first poem, *Rhyme of Whimsy*.

The stanza that follows is not quite as simple, where Ray talks about "Darkness covered by the light" instead of the other way around. It does become simple, however, if darkness is seen to represent satire; light, the humorous verse that covers it. "So fragrant – bells peal delight" (in the original Bengali: 'bells peal in – or because of – its fragrance') now makes perfect sense, if Ray meant to say that the verse will set off bells when we sniff its fragrant inner meanings out.

The implication in the lines that follow is towards the inevitable. "Fancy's envoys" convey tidings that "the five elements" will soon take the stage. The five elements, in Hinduism (and Brahmoism – Ray was a Brahmo), being Earth, Fire, Air, Water and Ether. In Hindu belief, everything is made up of these five elements. A person, upon death, is assimilated back into these five elements. Consider, however, the possible covert meaning, namely that the envoys are none other than the words of Ray's fancy. When they convey their inner meanings, the *five ghosts*– this time representing the collective ghosts (after all, they *are* invisible in his poems!) of all that he has so far mocked, are displayed dancing on stage for everyone to see.

No direct clues are available as to what the greedy elephants represent and why they might be suspended in the air with their legs upended. One possible guess at implied meaning is that they represent Ray's inner desire to continue to pen hilarious nonsense verse. The elephants are greedy because Ray would like to continue his work but knows he has very little time. Those desires are now suspended, upended; i.e., he is in no position to proceed and follow-through with his wishes. Ironically enough – and this would be appreciated only by those who can read the original verse in Bengali – the actual language used could, in double-entendre, also stand for the elephants having put one foot forward to begin a journey towards 'nothingness'. In *triple*-entendre, though, if the greedy elephants represent people and things Ray has mocked, then they are well and truly upended by the time he is done with his commentary on them.

"Rides Pegasus Grand Queen-Bee," in the original, is extremely cryptic. The original line comprises literally two words with no punctuation in between: 'Queen-Bee Pegasus –'. The meaning that this translator is guessing at is that Queen-Bee represents Ray's inner muse. The imagery: that she has either transformed into a winged horse and flown away, or ridden off on a winged-horse is, perhaps, Ray's way of implying that despite his desire to write, his muse has left him, and he can no longer find inspiration to pen more of his nonsense verse. Or it could be affirmation that Queen-Bee has shown her true colors in the hidden satire and revealed the Pegasus that she really is.

The naughty kid who today is quiet, obviously refers to Ray himself.

The reference to "horse-eggs bunched in bouquet new" may require a little more explanation. In Bengali, the epithet *horse-eggs* is used to refer to impossible or useless objects. Overtly, by implication, this may be a self-deprecating metaphor by Ray for his 'weird and absurd' nonsense verse. Or covertly, he may have meant that in the compilation Abol Tabol, he has bundled all the 'horse-eggs' that he has mocked so far in satire, into a bunch or bouquet. An additional implied interpretation that has also been suggested* is that on the eve of Ray's death, the horse-eggs represent the empty nature of human existence no matter how well lived (tied up nicely with string).

After this brief flash of spirit like that of a candle-flame flickering brightest just prior to dying out, Ray, however, slows down the tempo and the style of language from the fast and aggressive, to slow and mellow. The falling of a "timeless chill lunar dew", though, could imply just as well the clammy fingers of approaching death, as it could point, covertly, to 'timeless, cold irony'. The "drowsiness [that] doth sleep impend" invokes a rather obvious metaphor for impending death. Finally, Ray acknowledges in his last line that his "melodious muse is at an end."

Few, if any, have been so fortunate as to possess the ability to summarily chronicle in metaphor their own life, countenancing with composure its impending passing with such courageous combination of mischief and equanimity, in verse laden with scintillating humor, and rhymes of whimsy that have endured for generations.

I can imagine no finer epitaph.

---

* by Somnath Bhattacharyya, Kolkata, India.

Timeline of First-Publish Dates of the Poems and Potential Historical Events Commented Upon in the Poems

Year	English Title	Commentary (approximate first-publish period)
1915	Mutant Medley	Social commentary. No specific event recognized.
1916	Knotty Woodoo	British recruitment of Indian soldiers for the World War I effort, 1914.
1916	Mouche Filch	Social, and possible political, commentary. No specific event recognized.
1917	Battle Crazed	Commentary on heroism of Indian soldiers on the Western Front. World War I. 1914-1915.
1917	Ticking Old-Timer	Potentially, satire about British anti-sedition propaganda World War I.
1917	Butting Muse	Potentially, the shelling of the Indian city of Madras by German light cruiser SMS Emden, September 1914.
1918	The Contraption	Commentary on W. Heath Robinson's war cartoons, depicting outlandish mechanical inventions, during World War I.
1917	Shadow Play	Social commentary. No specific event recognized.
1917	Pumpkin-Pudge	Socio-political commentary. Possibly about investiture of new Viceroy Chelmsford.
1917	The Quack	Potential commentary on young British recruits to the Indian Civil Service.
1918	Caution	Social commentary. No specific event recognized.
1918	Hookah-Faror Hyangla	Socio-political commentary. No specific event recognized.
1918	Ding-a-ling and Dong	Commentary / satire not recognized.
1918	Neighbors	Possible political commentary on Lucknow Pact between Indian National Congress and Muslim League.
1919	That's a Problem!	Potential commentary on Encyclopedia Britannica
1919	To Catch a Thief	Potential socio-political commentary. Unrecognized.
1919	Ghostly Play	Commentary on Indian art; Bengali-school.
1919	The Ramgorur Kid	Potential commentary of serious demeanor of Brahmo Samaj Leadership.
1919	Fear Not	Political commentary on British Secretary of State for India, Edwin Montagu.
1919	Palm-Mystery	Social commentary. No specific event recognized.
1920	Wacky No-One	Social commentary. No specific event recognized.
1920	Once Bitten Twice Shy	Potential political commentary on the presence of British colonizers on India.
1920	Derelict Shack	Social or potentially political commentary. Unrecognized.
1920	Explanations	Potential social commentary. Unrecognized.
1920	The Delighted	Political commentary on 3 Indian statesmen, popularly known as Lal-Bal-Pal.
1920	Cry-Kid	Potential political commentary. Unrecognized.
1921	Missed!	Potential commentary on the accidental death of magician 'Chung Ling Soo' on stage.
1921	The Tomcat's Song	Potential political commentary. Unrecognized.
1921	The Daredevils	Political commentary on US reaction to Treaty of Versailles.
1921	Learning Science	Political commentary on the Sadler Commission Report on University of Calcutta, 1919.
1921	Notebook	Potential social or potentially political commentary. Unrecognized.
1921	Word-fancy-boughboomi	Possible commentary on equivocation by the british administration.
1922	Babu- The Snake Charmer	Political commentary. No specific event recognized.
1922	Crass Cow	Social commentary. No specific event recognized.
1921	The Twenty-One Law	Political commentary, Rowlatt Act.
1922	King of Bombogarh	Potential commentary on Maharaja Jai Singh of Alwar
1922	That's a Surprise!	Social commentary. No specific event recognized.
1922	It's All Good	Potential political commentary. No specific event recognized.
1923	Strongman	Potential commentary on the death of Indian wrestler Bhim Bhabani.
1923 (date estimated)	Sense of Essence	Political commentary, The Honors Scandal - English Parliament, 1922

Year columns across the top span 1915, 1916, 1917, 1918, 1919, 1920, 1921, 1922, 1923, each subdivided into months J F M A M J J A S O N D.

Note: The first-publish dates of 39 poems are definitely known. The date for *Sense of Essence* is estimated. First-publish dates of the other poems of Abol Tabol are unknown.

For a downloadable, high-resolution image, visit: https://en.wikipedia.org/wiki/Abol_Tabol

First-Publication Dates

(39 poems where first-publication dates are definitely known.)

Bengali Title	Year	Month	English Title
Khichuri	1915	Jan-Feb	Mutant Medley
Katth Buro		Feb-Mar	Knotty Woodoo
Gnof Churi		Mar-Apr	Mouche Filch
Lorai Khyapa		Apr-May	Battle Crazed
Katukutu Buro		May-Jun	Tickling Old-Timer
Gaaner Gnuto		Aug-Sep	Butting Muse
Khuror Kol	1916	Feb-Mar	The Contraption
Chhayabaji		Jun-Jul	Shadow Play
Kumropotash		Jul-Aug	Pumpkin-Pudge
Hatourey		Aug-Sep	The Quack
Shabdhan		Nov-Dec	Caution
Hnuko-Mukho...	1917	Mar-Apr	Hookah-Face ...
Dnaare-Dnaare ...		Jun-Jul	Ding-a-ling ...
Narod! Narod!		Sep-Oct	Neighbors
Ki Mushkil!	1918	Jan-Feb	That's a Problem!
Chor Dhora		Mar-Apr	To Catch a Thief
Bhooturey Khela		Apr-May	Ghostly Play
Ramgorurer ...		May-Jun	The *Ramgorur* Kid
Bhoy Peona		Jun-Jul	Fear Not
Haat Gonona		Jul-Aug	Palm-Mystery
Kimbhoot		Sep-Oct	Wacky No-One
Nera Beltolaay ...		Nov-Dec	Once Bitten Twice Shy
Burir Baari		Dec-Jan	Derelict Shack
Bujhiye Bola	1919	Jan-Feb	Explanations

233

Bengali Title	Year	Month	English Title
Ahlaadi	1919	Feb-Mar	The Delighted
Knaduney		Apr-May	Cry-Kid
Foshke Gelo!		May-Jun	Missed!
Hulor Gaan		Jul-Aug	The Tomcat's Song
Daanpitey		Aug-Sep	The Daredevils
Bigyan Shikkha		Sep-Oct	Learning Science
Noteboi	1920	Apr-May	Notebook
Shobdokolpo...		Sep-Oct	Word-Fancy...
Babu... Shapurey	1921	Jun-Jul	Babu Snake-Charmer
Tnyash Goru	1922	Feb-Mar	Crass Cow
Ekushey Aeen		Aug-Sep	The Twenty-One Law
Bombagarer Raja		Oct-Nov	King of *Bombagarh*
Awbaak Kando		Oct-Nov	What a Surprise!
Bhalo re Bhalo	1923	May-Jun	It's All Good
Palowan		Aug-Sep	Strongman

Bengali-English Title Cross-Reference

(In alphabetical order of Bengali titles.)

236

Notes

(Source medium 'print' unless mentioned otherwise.)

Book One

1. Chaudhuri, Sukanta. *The Select Nonsense of Sukumar Ray*, Oxford University Press, 2010, 44
2. Asbury, Herbert. *The Barbary Coast. An Informal History of the San Francisco Underworld*, Alfred A. Knopf, New York, 1933, 150-164
3. Indian Charivari, February 20, 1874, 39

Book Two

1. Ray, Sukumar. *'Abol Tabol' Sukumar Sahitya Samagra,* 1973. Vol 1. Ed. Satyajit Ray and Partha Basu. [published in Bengali] Kolkata: Ananda Publishers, 2014, 314
2. Ibid., 314
3. Chakraborty, Punyalata. *Chhelebelar Dinguli* (Childhood Days), [published in Bengali] Newscript, Calcutta, 1958, 92
4. Sengoopta, Chandak. *The Rays Before Satyajit*, Oxford University Press, 2016, 312
5. Goswami, Supriya. *Colonial India in Children's Literature*, Routledge, 2012, 152
6. Bhadury, Poushali. *Fantastic Beasts and How to Sketch Them: The Fabulous Bestiary of Sukumar Ray*, South Asian Review, Vol. 34, No. 1, 2013, 18-21
7. Omissi, David. *The Sepoy and the Raj – The Indian Army, 1860-1940,* Macmillan Press, 1998, 1-46
8. Padmanabha, P. *Indian Census and Anthropological Investigations,* X^{th} *International Congress of Anthropological and Ethnological Sciences*, 1978, 6
9. Bates, Crispin. *Race, Caste and Tribe in Central India: the early origins of Indian anthropometry,* in Robb, Peter. *The Concept of Race in South Asia.* Delhi, Oxford University Press, 1995, 238
10. Padmanabha, P. Ibid. (8), 4
11. Ray, Sukumar. *Sukumar Sahitya Samagra,* 1973. Vol 3. Ed. Satyajit Ray and Partha Basu. [published in Bengali] Kolkata: Ananda Publishers, 2014, 293
12. Dadabhoy, Bakhtiar. *Barons of Banking,* Random House India, 2013, 344
13. Ray, Sukumar. Ibid. (11), 296-297

14. Basu, Shrabani. *For King and Another Country – Indian Soldiers on the Western Front*, Bloomsbury, 2015, 196
15. Tharoor, Shashi. *Why the Indian soldiers of WW1 were forgotten*, BBC Magazine. July 2, 2015, Internet: http://www.bbc.com/news/magazine-33317368
16. Sengoopta, Chandak. Ibid. (4), 312
17. Sen, Satadru. *Disciplined Natives – Race, Freedom and Confinement in Colonial India*, Primus Books, New Delhi, 2012, 27
18. Maiti, Abhik. *The Nonsense World of Sukumar Roy* [recte *Ray*]: *The Influence of British Colonialism on Sukumar Roy's* [recte *Ray's*] *Nonsense Poems – With Special Reference to Abol Tabol*, International Journal of English Language, Literature and Translation Studies (IJELR), Vol. 3. Issue 2, 2016, 446
19. Tharoor, Shashi. *The Un-Indian Civil Service*, Open magazine, August 12, 2016, Internet: http://www.openthemagazine.com/article/essay/the-un-indian-civil-service
20. Maiti, Abhik. Ibid. (18), 444
21. Goswami, Supriya. Ibid. (5), 155
22. Chaudhuri, Sukanta. *The Select Nonsense of Sukumar Ray*, Oxford University Press, 2010, 22
23. Goswami, Supriya. Ibid. (5), 156
24. Dhillon, Amrit. *Bejewelled Carriageways*, The Telegraph U.K., Oct 16, 2004. Internet: http://www.telegraph.co.uk/expat/4193893/Bejewelled-carriageways.html
25. Ray, Sukumar. Ibid. (11), 304
26. Goswami, Supriya. Ibid. (5), 155-156
27. Purcell, Hugo. *The Maharajah of Bikaner*, Haus Publishing, London, 2010, 'Prologue:1919', xiii
28. Chaudhuri, Sukanta. *The World of Sukumar Ray* in *Telling Tales: Children's Literature in India*, Ed. Amit Dasgupta. New Age International Publishers Ltd. Wiley Eastern Ltd. New Delhi, India 1995, 88-96.
29. Schauffler, Robert Haven. *Flag day; its history*, Moffat, Yard and Co. New York, 1912, 145
30. Follet, Ken. *Fall of Giants*, Dutton, New York, 2010, 913
31. Sykes, Charles H. *Cartoons Magazine* Vol. 7, Iss. 4, April 1914, 496
32. Ray, Sukumar. Ibid. (11), 174
33. Robinson, Andrew. *Selected Letters of Sukumar Ray,* South Asia Research, Vol.7, No.2, November 1987, 179
34. Mitter, Partha. *Art and Nationalism in Colonial India 1850-1922 Occidental Orientations*, Cambridge University Press, 1994, 360-361

35. Ibid., 368
36. Ibid., 368
37. Ibid., 371
38. Ibid., 361
39. Maiti, Abhik. Ibid. (18), 446
40. Paris, Matthew. *Great Parliamentary Scandals*, Robson Books, London, 1995, 89
41. Ibid., 90
42. Taylor, A.J.P. *English History 1914-1945*, Oxford University Press, 1990, 188
43. Ray, Sukumar. Ibid. (11), 311
44. Neate, Bobbie. *Conspiracy of Secrets*, John Blake, 2012, 275
45. Kaminsky, Arnold P. *The India Office 1880-1910*, Greenwood Press, Connecticut, 1986, 37
46. Maiti, Abhik. Ibid. (18), 445-446
47. Basu, Abanindrakirshna. *Bangalir Circus* (The Bengalee's Circus) [published in Bengali] First Ed. July 2013, Gangchil, Kolkata, 165-169
48. Gupta, Abhijit. *Man who lifted elephants*, The Telegraph, India, July 18, 2010. Internet: https://www.telegraphindia.com/1100718/jsp/calcutta/story_12691629.jsp
49. Majumdar, Bijayaratna. *Bangali-Bir Bhim Bhavani* (Bengalee-Hero Bhim Bhavani) [published in Bengali] in Manasi O Marmabani (Bhaadra 1329), 19
50. Ghosh, Anilchandra. *Byaame Bangali* (The Bengalee in Gymnastics and Exercise) [published in Bengali] 9th Ed. 1927, Presidency Library, Calcutta, 14-18
51. Majumdar, Bijayaratna. Ibid. (49), 16
52. Lourdusamy, J. *Science and National Consciousness in Bengal 1870-1930*, Orient Longman, New Delhi, 2004, 210-11
53. Stahl, Christopher, *Outdoing Ching Ling Foo*, in Hass, L., Coppa, F., Peck, J. (Eds.). *Performing Magic on the Western Stage. From the Eighteenth Century to the Present.* Palgrave Macmillan (US), 2008, 151
54. Wikipedia. Chung Ling Soo. Internet: https://en.wikipedia.org/wiki/Chung_Ling_Soo
55. Ray, Sukumar. Ibid. (1), 314

Bibliography

Asbury, Herbert. *The Barbary Coast. An Informal History of the San Francisco Underworld*, Alfred A. Knopf, New York, 1933

Basu, Abanindrakirshna. *Bangalir Circus* (The Bengali's Circus) [published in Bengali] First Ed. July 2013, Gangchil, Kolkata

Basu, Shrabani. *For King and Another Country – Indian Soldiers on the Western Front*, Bloomsbury, 2015

Bates, Crispin. *Race, Caste and Tribe in Central India: the early origins of Indian anthropometry*, in Robb, Peter. *The Concept of Race in South Asia*, Delhi, Oxford University Press, 1995

Baum, L. Frank. *The Wonderful Wizard of Oz*, George M. Hill Company, Chicago, 1900

Bhadury, Poushali. *Fantastic Beasts and How to Sketch Them: The Fabulous Bestiary of Sukumar Ray*, South Asian Review, Vol. 34, No. 1, 2013

Bhattacharyya, Priyadarshini. *Tracing the 'Sense' behind 'Nonsense': A comparative study of selected texts of Sukumar Ray and Edward Lear*, International Journal of English Language, Literature and Humanities, Vol. II, Iss. X, February, 2015

Chakraborty, Punyalata. *Chhelebelar Dinguli* (Childhood Days), [published in Bengali] Newscript, Calcutta, 1958

Chaudhuri, Sukanta. *The Select Nonsense of Sukumar Ray*, Oxford University Press, 2010

Chaudhuri, Sukanta. *The World of Sukumar Ray* in *Telling Tales: Children's Literature in India*, Ed. Amit Dasgupta. New Age International Publishers Ltd. Wiley Eastern Ltd. New Delhi, India 1995

Dadabhoy, Bakhtiar. *Barons of Banking*, Random House India, 2013

Dhillon, Amrit, *Bejewelled Carriageways*, The Telegraph, U.K., 2004

Follet, Ken. *Fall of Giants*, Dutton, New York, 2010

Ghosh, Anilchandra. *Byaame Bangali* (The Bengali in Gymnastics and Exercise) [published in Bengali] 9th Ed. 1927, Presidency Library, Calcutta

Goswami, Supriya. *Colonial India in Children's Literature,* Routledge, 2012

Gupta, Abhijit. *Man who lifted elephants*, The Telegraph, India, July 18, 2010

Indian Charivari, February 20, 1874

Lourdusamy, J. *Science and National Consciousness in Bengal 1870-1930,* Orient Longman, New Delhi, 2004

Kaminsky, Arnold P. *The India Office 1880-1910*, Greenwood Press, Connecticut, 1986

Maiti, Abhik. *The Nonsense World of Sukumar Roy* [recte *Ray*]: *The Influence of British Colonialism on Sukumar Roy's* [recte *Ray's*] *Nonsense Poems – With Special Reference to Abol-Tabol*, International Journal of English Language, Literature and Translation Studies (IJELR), Vol. 3. Issue 2, 2016

Majumdar, Bijayaratna. *Bangali-Bir Bhim Bhavani* (Bengali-Hero Bhim Bhavani) [published in Bengali] in Manasi O Marmabani (Bhaadra 1329)

Mitter, Partha. *Art and Nationalism in Colonial India 1850-1922 Occidental Orientations*, Cambridge University Press, 1994

Neate, Bobbie. *Conspiracy of Secrets*, John Blake, 2012

Omissi, David. *The Sepoy and the Raj – The Indian Army, 1860-1940,* Macmillan Press, 1998

Padmanabha, P. *Indian Census and Anthropological Investigations,* X^{th} *International Congress of Anthropological and Ethnological Sciences*, 1978

Paris, Matthew. *Great Parliamentary Scandals*, Robson Books, London, 1995

Purcell, Hugo. *The Maharajah of Bikaner*, Haus Publishing, London, 2010

Ray, Sukumar. *'Abol Tabol' Sukumar Sahitya Samagra, 1973. Vol 1-3.* Ed. Satyajit Ray and Partha Basu. Kolkata: Ananda Publishers, 2014

Robinson, Andrew. *Selected Letters of Sukumar Ray*, South Asia Research, Vol.7, No.2, November 1987

Schauffler, Robert Haven. *Flag day; its history*, Moffat, Yard and Co. New York, 1912

Sen, Satadru. *Disciplined Natives – Race, Freedom and Confinement in Colonial India* (Primus Books, New Delhi, 2012)

Sengoopta, Chandak. *The Rays Before Satyajit*, Oxford University Press, 2016

Stahl, Christopher, *Outdoing Ching Ling Foo*, in Hass, L., Coppa, F., Peck, J. (Eds.). *Performing Magic on the Western Stage. From the Eighteenth Century to the Present*. Palgrave Macmillan (US), 2008

Sykes, Charles H. Cartoons Magazine Vol. 7, Iss. 4, April 1914

Taylor, A.J.P. *English History 1914-1945*, Oxford University Press, 1990

Tharoor, Shashi. *Why the Indian soldiers of WW1 were forgotten,* BBC Magazine, July 2015

Tharoor, Shashi. *The Un-Indian Civil Service*, Open magazine, August 12, 2016

Telegraph, The UK Oct 16, 2004. Internet.

Walsh, Ben. *GCSE Modern World History*, John Murray, London, 1996

About the Author

Sukumar Ray (1887-1923) was a prolific Indian writer, poet and playwright. He was one of the first writers of nonsense verse in Bengali, for children.

Son of children's fiction writer Upendrakishore Ray Chowdhury, Sukumar graduated with honors in physics and chemistry from Presidency College, Calcutta (now Kolkata), and trained in photography and printing technology at the London County Council School of Photo-Engraving and Lithography, and the Manchester School of Technology in England.

He developed new methods of halftone block-making and was also elected Fellow of the Royal Photographic Society. He is the father of internationally acclaimed Indian filmmaker Satyajit Ray.

After Upendrakishore's death in 1915, Sukumar Ray assumed the editorship of children's magazine *Sandesh* started by his father and remained editor until his own untimely death.

About the Translator

Niladri Roy is a self-described dyed-in-the-wool Bengali, with varied interests.

An engineer by training from Bengal Engineering College, Sibpur, in India, he is a full-time practicing technologist based in Silicon Valley, California. His interests, outside of his profession and occasional experimentation with writing, include photography, piloting single-engine aircraft and high-altitude trekking in the Sierras, Himalayas and equatorial Africa. He is the author of the book *Everest Base Camp Trek – Kathmandu and the Ascent of Kala Patthar* (Blurb, San Francisco, 2008).

Roy, a naturalized American, was born in Assam, India, to Bengali parents, grew up near Kolkata, and emigrated to the United States in the mid-1990s.

For matters relating to this book, he can be reached at: rhymesofwhimsy@gmail.com.

Prefer to read the poems in the Bengali original,
side-by-side with their English translations?

Rhymes of Whimsy – Abol Tabol Dual-Language Edition

Close on the heels of the original *Rhymes of Whimsy – The Complete Abol
Tabol,* follows, by popular demand, the dual-language edition *with side by
side Bengali originals* and their English translations.

Formatted to enable effortless at-a-glance comparison of each original line
with its English translation, this edition offers twice the enjoyment, twice
the fun, and is a fabulous learning tool for children.

Color glossy cover, black-and-white interior, 8.5" x 11", 80 pages, with
more than 40 illustrations.

Published by Haton Cross Press.
Available for purchase online, or wherever great books are sold.

Facebook: https://facebook.com/rhymesofwhimsy

Printed in Great Britain
by Amazon

32486736R00144